I've travelled the world twice over,
Met the famous: saints and sinners,
Poets and artists, kings and queens,
Old stars and hopeful beginners,
I've been where no-one's been before,
Learned secrets from writers and cooks
All with one library ticket
To the wonderful world of books.

© JANICE JAMES.

HUNTER IN THE DARK

Philip Blair, blind for the past two years, has newly returned to his profession as a teacher when he becomes 'witness' to murder. Angered that the killer contemptuously regarded him as harmless because he was blind, and frustrated by police disregard for his theories, Philip sets out on his own investigation. As he struggles to find some answers, it suddenly becomes clear that a child's life is at stake, and Philip himself may be in deadly danger — a blind man in confrontation with a determined killer.

ESTELLE THOMPSON

◆

HUNTER IN THE DARK

Complete and Unabridged

ULVERSCROFT
Leicester

First published in Great Britain in 1978 by
Robert Hale Limited
London

First Large Print Edition
published 1996
by arrangement with
Robert Hale Limited
London

British Library CIP Data

Thompson, Estelle
    Hunter in the dark.—Large print ed.—
Ulverscroft large print series: mystery
I. Title
823 [F]

ISBN 0–7089–3472–2

Published by
F. A. Thorpe (Publishing) Ltd.
Anstey, Leicestershire
Set by Words & Graphics Ltd.
Anstey, Leicestershire
Printed and bound in Great Britain by
T. J. Press (Padstow) Ltd., Padstow, Cornwall

This book is printed on acid-free paper

1

HE turned right at the corner at the bottom of the hill and walked north in the pitch darkness with the sun on his right cheek.

That was one of the things he hadn't got used to, not in two years: the sun warm on his face, and not the faintest ghost of light in the darkness.

But he wasn't thinking of that very much this morning. He was tense and a little excited. If he hadn't been fully concentrated on what he was doing he'd have been sardonically amused at that: getting excited over catching the bus to work.

He felt the warmth of the sun leave his cheek and he knew he'd stepped into the early-morning shadow the hill flung over the footpath and part of the roadway that had been chopped into its foot. He knew as well as if he could see them that there were houses on top of the hill above the rocky embankment — neat suburban houses in pleasant small suburban gardens. There were even trees — eucalypts with cool grey trunks, and other trees he didn't know; or didn't remember from that other world.

Up there on the hill he could hear a magpie singing, the notes so pure he smiled.

But he didn't stop counting. One hundred and sixteen paces from the corner, walking rather slowly, trying to walk confidently, fighting the urge to grope the space ahead with his cane. He wondered grimly whether one ever left behind that fear of walking into something, or someone.

He listened with fierce concentration for the sound of approaching footsteps, but he seemed to be alone on the footpath. Desultory early traffic was increasing, and though this wasn't an arterial road into the City it was much busier and noisier than the street his flat was in.

He kept the tip of his white cane lightly on the edge of the kerbing, feeling for the landmarks he'd so doggedly memorized.

The light-pole on the corner, twenty-three paces to the fire-hydrant, then ninety-three to the yellow and black bus-stop marker post. Were they still yellow and black? He must ask someone sometime.

He heard footsteps coming toward him, and two male voices discussing football. Don't hesitate, he told himself; keep walking. He heard the voices pause and guessed he was being scrutinized curiously, but the steps passed on.

Ninety, ninety-one. A moment's near-panic. Suppose he'd lost count, suppose he'd missed touching the post —

The cane contacted something, and with a determined effort at a casual gesture he put out a hand and felt it rest on the pyramid top of the bus-stop post.

He put down his brief-case against his right foot and felt for his handkerchief, his palms and upper lip damp with sweat. He wiped his face, felt if his tie was straight, and stood quietly, relaxing. Phase one, he told himself with a tiny smile.

Traffic passed fairly constantly, and

twice there were snatches of conversation from passing pedestrians, but there was no chatter from people at the bus-stop. He wondered if he was the only passenger waiting. He fancied after a few minutes that there was someone else there — thought he heard slight movements: a shoe scraped on the pavement, the rustle of clothing.

Experimentally, he said:

"Excuse me, are you waiting for a Terrace bus?"

There was a moment's silence and then a child's voice — a little girl's — said a trifle reluctantly: "Yes."

He heard the reluctance. "I'm sorry to bother you, but I wonder if you'd mind telling me when it comes? You see, I'm blind."

"Oh." She seemed to think about it for a minute, sizing him up carefully. Then: "Where are you going?"

"St Stephen's School. I'm a history teacher there."

"Are you?" She sounded interested, her suspicions allayed. "But how can you teach if you're blind?"

He smiled. "I'm not awfully sure yet.

4

I've only just begun. I used to teach before I was blind."

She was silent again for a minute. He wondered how old she was — ten or twelve, probably.

"Is that why the other man came with you yesterday morning and all last week? Because you're blind?"

"Yes."

"How come he didn't come this morning?"

"I didn't want him to. He teaches at the same school, and he picked me up from home in his car each morning for the first two weeks after I started work. But that means he has to come a long way, so I got him to help me practise walking to the stop and home again. I felt that by today I could do it myself. It seems a bit silly to think a grown man can't catch a bus by himself, doesn't it?"

"Is that why you're so early for the bus? You started off from home a long time before you need have?"

"Yes, I guess I did. I wanted to allow time in case I got a bit lost."

"What would you do if you did get

5

lost?" she demanded anxiously.

"I'd meet someone pretty soon, and ask directions." He held up his white cane. "People know from this that I'm blind."

His companion heaved a sigh. "My mother always makes me leave home miles too early," she said sadly. "I wish she didn't *fuss* so. Does your mother make you leave too early, too?"

He chuckled. He was going to enjoy mornings waiting for the bus in the company of this young lady.

Before he could answer, a man's voice said, "Hello, Linda. Looks as though there's going to be a shower. Hop in — I'm passing the school."

There had been the sound of a car pulling into the kerb, but in the pattern of traffic noises it hadn't really registered.

"Oh, hello. Thank you," the little girl said.

He felt a light touch on his arm. "Will you be all right if it rains?"

"Sure," he told her, touched by her concern.

"Well," she said, "ask Mr Giordano about the bus. You'll know when he

6

comes — he smokes cigars."

He laughed. "Thank you very much. I'll meet you again tomorrow."

He heard the car door open and shut and the car pull away, and felt at once cheered and suddenly very alone again.

He thought about the weather. Blast, he'd forgotten to listen to the forecast and hadn't brought a coat. He touched his watch whose special face told his fingers that it was about time for the bus anyway.

There were children's voices now — two boys arguing about last night's television programmes — and they halted at the bus-stop with the sound of school-cases being put down unceremoniously on the footpath; a moment's silence as they apparently summed up the man who stood with one hand on the post, and then their talk resumed.

There was a click of heels and a wisp of perfume: typist on the way to the office. Then a heavy step and the unmistakeable smell of a cigar.

"Mr Giordano?"

"Yeah," a man's voice said suspiciously.

"My name's Philip Blair. Would you

7

mind telling me when a Terrace bus comes? I'm blind."

"Okay, mister." There was a pause. Then: "Well how in hell did you know who I am?"

Philip smiled. "There was a little girl here when I arrived. I asked her to tell me about the bus, but someone picked her up in a car a while ago. She said to ask you when you came. She said I'd know you because you smoke cigars. Very good ones, I may add," he lied courteously.

"What the hell has — Oh. Oh, I see: you can smell the cigar?"

"Yes."

"Hey, that's pretty smart," Mr Giordano decided, a deep laugh melting his suspicions. "Of course, I've always heard that people like you have better hearing and everything than people who can see."

Philip had heard it, too, but before he could comment Mr Giordano said:

"Here's our bus — Terrace, you said?" And he proceeded to direct Philip on board and talk to him about horse-racing all the way to his own stop, which was before Philip's.

"But don't you worry, mister. I'll tell

the driver to let you know when you get there. Excuse me, lady, how far are you goin'?"

A voice — elderly, pleasant — said a trifle reluctantly from across the aisle, "Right into town."

"Okay, you tell this gentleman when his stop comes up, will you?" And he hurried his large frame off the bus.

The elderly lady said nothing, and Philip sensed she was puzzled. Then as realization of his blindness dawned, she said quickly, "Certainly I'll be happy to tell you when we reach your stop. Where are you going?"

"St Stephen's School. Stop seven."

Presently she said, "But you should have someone looking after you. Why are you out alone?"

His mind flicked back over the ordeal of getting to the bus-stop, and finding there a twelve-year-old girl to whom catching the bus was a purely inconsequential routine.

He said with sudden savagery, "Because I'm a man, not a sickly brat, and I don't need anyone to look after me, thank you."

9

There was instant silence among the passengers around him, and he realized he must have spoken with sharp penetration, and he was at once ashamed.

"I'm sorry. That was unpardonable of me. And of course I — "

He stopped, somehow stubbornly unable to make the admission that in fact he must have someone 'looking after' him much of the time. At this moment he was dependent on the lady herself, and the driver — if Mr Giordano had remembered to tell him to tell Philip when they reached the St Stephen's stop.

After a brief moment the elderly lady said with, Philip was sure, a smile, "It's all right. I was being tactless and interfering. And I shan't turn nasty and refuse to tell you when we get to St Stephen's. Will you tell me why you're going there?"

And she chatted amicably and interestedly with him till the bus reached the school.

To his surprise it was the Principal, not Robert Henderson, who was waiting to meet him.

"Well, well! Managing splendidly, aren't you?"

Trevor Markham was a big man with a heavy voice who, Philip knew, had vigorously opposed the appointment of a blind man to his staff and could never speak to Philip without sounding patronising in spite of — or perhaps because of — his attempts at hearty approval.

"Robert phoned to say he was ill," Markham went on, "so I thought I'd better make sure for myself that you were all right. I can see you're doing marvellously — inspiration to us all, I'm sure."

"Thank you," Philip said hollowly. "I'm sorry Robert's ill."

"Yes. Asthma giving him trouble. Good chap, Henderson." There was just a moment's pause. "You'd have been hard pressed to manage without him here, wouldn't you?"

"Yes," Philip admitted at once. "Yes, I would. Robert or someone like him."

"I suppose," Markham went on as he walked with Philip up to the staff-room door, "his own handicap makes him more sensitive to the problems of other handicapped people. Though of

11

course deafness isn't as big a problem as loss of sight. And that impressive hearing-aid he wears helps, no doubt. I thought these days they'd done away with all those cords and batteries that make hearing-aids so obvious."

The Principal was over-talking in the manner of a man who wants to say something and is reluctant to begin. Philip waited.

"And — ah — how do you feel about your job?" Markham asked. "Any special problems? Any more trouble with Taylor?"

"Nothing I haven't been able to cope with, sir."

James Taylor was a senior student who had set out from the beginning to deliberately disrupt Philip's classes by taking advantage of his blindness.

"If you have trouble with him, Philip, report to me. The boy's a born trouble-maker."

"He's just a spoiled brat who likes to feel important," Philip said. "I think by letting him have his head he's already proved to the others that he's behaving childishly, and he'll soon prove it to himself. He's a young man with a brilliant mind, if he decides to use it."

"I still feel I should take him out of your classes."

"No!" Philip said sharply. "That would be capitulation to petty bullying, and Taylor and I would both be the losers."

"Nasty streak of viciousness in the boy — must be, to take advantage of a man's handicap."

"Maybe," Philip said. "But Taylor has a passion for excelling, at his studies or anywhere else. He wants the best possible of everything, including teachers. He doesn't want me because he shares your feeling that a blind man can't teach a sighted class."

Markham's head jerked in surprise and he frowned. "Have I ever said that?"

"Not to me," Philip said drily.

"I'm prepared," the Principal said stiffly, "to wait and see."

"Thank you, sir," Philip said. "So am I."

★ ★ ★

In all, it was a satisfactory day. Classes went well enough, Taylor was absent, another teacher saw him on to the bus after he refused the tentative offer: "I suppose it's no use offering to drive you home, you mule" — and the bus-driver told him when his stop was reached.

Philip stood on the pavement while the bus pulled away. "Post's about four feet to your left, mate," the driver had told him in answer to his question. He touched it now with his cane, then walked on, counting steps, till the cane found the pedestrian-crossing post. He listened carefully to the traffic, for this crossing was a zebra-stripe, not controlled by lights. He wondered whether the driver of that truck that stopped routinely for him had the vaguest notion of what it was like to be trapped in a flimsy cage of darkness, hearing several tons of steel and glass and rubber bearing down from somewhere not quite pin-pointable.

As he stepped on to the footpath he realized he was sweating a little and he took off his jacket as he turned south with the westering sun almost hot now on this bit of street that had been in the shadow of the hill this morning. He reflected that autumn, certainly in Queensland, was far the most pleasant time of the year.

That threatened shower hadn't materialized, he remembered — at least not before the bus came — and he smiled as he thought of his young friend of the morning, picturing her watching interestedly for him tomorrow.

As he turned in off the street to walk along the path to his front door, a woman's voice, deep and husky, spoke to him.

"Hello, Philip."

The voice caressed the last word, and his mouth twitched in a half-amused downturn at one corner. This was one day he could do without Marcia Feldman.

"I've waited an hour," she told him, "just filling in the time weeding the garden till you came home. I've been so anxious that the day *had* to go well with you. It did, didn't it?"

"Yes," he nodded. "It did. That is to say, I didn't fall flat on my face in the street, spill a glass of water over my desk, or forget to wipe the egg off my face after breakfast. Whether I can really usefully teach is something else."

"Of course you can." She came close to him and took his arm and he felt the warmth and strength of her tall slender body. The voice, the woman, oozed confidence. He wondered how you could ever be sure, with a second-rate actress like Marcia who never stopped playing to the gallery, what was stage-play and what was genuine feeling; unless you knew her very well. On the whole, he doubted whether Marcia — who, in private life Mrs Max Walsh, shared one of the other flats in the building with her insurance-salesman husband — had much in the way of genuine feelings. But it would be very hard to get behind Marcia's carefully-designed facade.

He disengaged his arm at the front door and said good night. Marcia alternately amused and irritated him. This was one night he wasn't disposed to be amused.

He made himself a cup of tea, listened to the tape-recording he'd made of the day's classes, and prepared his evening meal with the necessary precision-movements and intense concentration.

As he ate, he listened to the evening

news, alertly prepared to pick up any points in current affairs which he could use to catch his classes' interest by inviting them to see history in the making.

National and overseas news disposed of, the reader in the Brisbane studio took up the State news with an instinctively grim note in his voice.

"Police throughout Queensland and interstate have been alerted in the search for a deranged murderer, following the accidental discovery by two City Council workmen this afternoon of the partly-clothed body of a twelve-year-old girl in bush near a side road on Mt Coot-tha. The body has been identified as that of Linda Benmore of Walton Hill."

2

THE news-reader went on to explain that when Linda didn't return home from school, her mother made enquiries at houses along the route to the bus-stop. No one had seen Linda this afternoon, but two or three people said they had seen her on her way to the bus this morning. Mrs Benmore had phoned the headmaster at the State school Linda attended, and he reported that she had not been at school. The frightened Mrs Benmore then phoned the police, and her husband at work.

Just before five o'clock the shocked Council workmen reported their grim find. The body was identified by Mr Ken Benmore, the father. The cause of death would not be known until a post-mortem examination had been carried out, but there were head injuries. A woman who worked at a milk-bar across the road from the bus-stop, and knew Linda by sight, had told police she saw a man in a car pick Linda up this morning while she was waiting for the bus.

Police were anxious to contact this man.

Police were also anxious to contact a man seen waiting at the bus-stop when Linda was picked up. Police wished to emphasize that no suspicion was attached to this man, as he was seen to be still there after Linda was driven away. But he might be able to give extremely valuable information about the driver of the car which picked Linda up. The man at the bus-stop was described as about five feet ten inches, or one hundred and eighty centimetres, tall; slim build, wearing a light-coloured suit and dark glasses.

Police appealed to this man to come forward.

The reader's voice went on to other news items, but Philip didn't hear. He sat stiffly, frozen in disbelief.

A car stopping at the kerb, a man's voice saying: "Hello, Linda," and something about a shower. Philip remembered, too, a small hand laid on his arm and a concerned young voice saying, "Will you

19

be all right if it rains?"

Philip crashed one clenched fist into the palm of his other hand in a fury of frustration. "Bloody murderer! Dirty bloody murderer!" he cried aloud.

He reached out and turned the radio off, then got up and went to the phone on the table by the kitchen bench, running his fingers lightly around the phone-dial to find the first space. He spun it three times and asked the prompt responder at the other end for the police.

He realized he was shaking a little, as if he'd been running, and breathing fast with shock and bitter anger — and grief.

Grief for a little girl concerned for a blind man who might be caught in the rain. A little girl intelligent enough to say: "Ask Mr Giordano about the bus. You'll know when he comes — he smokes cigars."

"Police here," a brisk voice said.

"My name is Philip Blair. I live at Paynton Street, Walton Hill." Even to himself, his voice sounded tight with anger. "I'm calling about the little girl who was murdered today — Linda someone — I just heard the radio news."

The voice asked courteously, "Would you hold the line a moment, sir? I'll put you on to someone in the homicide division connected with the case."

In a few seconds a voice whose terseness told it was already tired of time-wasting calls but knew routinely it would have to deal with many more, said, "Inspector Batlow."

Philip repeated his name and address. "I heard the radio news about the little girl, Linda — I don't recall the surname. I was the man at the bus-stop."

The inspector's voice instantly came alive with interest. "Indeed, Mr Blair. Thank you very much for calling promptly. Would you mind identifying the stop for me, just to make sure there's no mistake?"

"Twenty-eight. I was waiting for a Terrace bus."

"Thank you. You were there when the car picked up the little girl?"

"Yes."

"That's splendid. How close a description can you give us, sir? Of the car and the driver?"

"That's just it," Philip said bitterly. "That's why he had the nerve to pick her up right under my nose. He knew damned well I wouldn't give any description. I'm blind."

There was a dead silence and Philip could almost feel the detective's frustration.

"Oh. I'm sorry, Mr Blair. Yes, I see what you mean — the man felt he ran no risks. But perhaps he wasn't quite as right as he thought. I'll be out to talk to you almost immediately."

The inspector and another man introduced as Detective Sergeant Connor were at Philip's flat in twenty minutes. As they all sat down, Philip said, "I'm sorry, but I simply don't see how I can be of any real help. Neither," he added, "did he."

"There may be something, you know — something you heard, something that was said. If you'll just go over it — think of everything — every word that was said, if you can recall. It's surprising, sometimes, just what we do remember."

Philip said sharply, "But there was so little — it was all so quick — "

He gave his head a little shake. "Sorry,

22

Inspector. I don't believe I've ever felt quite so damned useless."

The inspector looked at him for a moment compassionately. But his tone was matter-of-fact. "Did you know Linda well, Mr Blair?"

"What?" Philip raised his head. "Oh. No, Inspector, I'd never met the child before. But I feel I did know her very well."

He told of his brief meeting with her, and the policeman nodded. "I think I can understand how you must feel. But you may be able to help a good deal more than you realize. You say, and it must be true, that the man dared to pick Linda up only because you are blind. That means it was someone who *knows* you're blind. Think carefully: could the voice have been the voice of someone you know?"

Philip shook his head. "I certainly didn't recognize it, but of course it could have been someone who knows me only slightly. Or it could just as easily have been a total stranger — anyone who has watched my colleague and me catching the bus over the past week, or anyone

23

who rode on the bus; or anyone who lives around here. I might very well never have heard the voice in my life."

Inspector Batlow rested his chin on his hands and looked at Philip thoughtfully.

"Was there anything distinctive about the voice: an accent, a peculiarity?"

Philip shook his head. "It was all so quick, so casual, so natural. I simply didn't take any particular notice."

The sergeant glanced down at his shorthand notes and said, "You seem to have remembered the exact words, Mr Blair: 'Hello, Linda. Looks as though there's going to be a shower. Hop in — I'm passing the school.' Just let yourself think back for a moment; try to *hear* the man say them again. Take your time."

Philip put his hands over his face and was quite still for half a minute. Then he dropped his hands.

"He sounded as if he had a cold," he said. "I'd forgotten, but the voice was blurred and a bit hoarse."

"That could possibly have been done to disguise the voice. Or it might just as easily have been genuine. Mr Blair," the

24

inspector said suddenly, getting up and pacing across the flat's small living-room, "how long have you been blind?"

"Two years."

"You've had specialist rehabilitation training?"

"Yes."

"Mr Blair, describe me."

Momentarily startled, Philip smiled faintly as he realized why the question had been asked. The inspector stayed still and silent.

Philip said slowly, "Australian born, aged about fifty. Height probably near six feet, fairly solid build, but not overweight, I should think — probably around fourteen stone. Non-smoker. How did I make out?"

"Australian born, aged fifty-two, height five feet ten, weight thirteen and a half stone. Non-smoker. Now tell me about the man in the car."

Philip frowned in concentration, silent.

"Height is next to impossible," he said presently, "because he was sitting down. So is build — I had no chance to hear how he moved. But — well, Australian born, age about thirty. Voice not so deep as yours, but not in any way shrill or efemenate — not even light in tone. In fact, I'd say it was the voice of a big man, but that's only a guess. I'd think he was a fairly well educated man — not the unskilled labourer type. The car — "

He rubbed his chin, trying to remember. "It was quiet — a late model, probably Falcon or Holden. But — that's not very helpful. I'm sorry."

"You're sure Linda didn't call him by name?"

"I'm sure. But I'm equally sure she knew him."

"You say *he* called *her* by name. You don't think that was enough to give you, and Linda also, the *impression* it was someone she knew? It might have been designed to trick her into trusting him."

"No." Philip shook his head positively. "There was a tone of recognition in Linda's voice. And — yes, I'm sure of it: surprise. She was surprised to see this person there, or surprised that he offered her a lift."

"She had no hesitation about riding with this man? There was nothing to suggest she was forced into the car, either physically or by some threat?"

"Not at all. I think she was pleased to see him, if anything. Certainly she had no doubts about riding with him."

"I see." The inspector nodded. "Well, thank you, Mr Blair. We'll give the child's parents your description of the man — see if it fits anyone they know. And, tomorrow, would you be kind enough to come around to the police headquarters and listen to a few tapes? We have some voices on tape of chaps who've been known to make obscene telephone calls — that kind of thing. Usually that type of offender stops there — satisfied with making a nuisance of himself, frightening or upsetting women. But occasionally they do more than that. There's just a faint chance you might pick a voice that sounds like the one you heard. Then we can check him out for yesterday. It's a very long shot, of course, but we try everything."

"Yes, of course." Philip hesitated. "Inspector, the news item mentioned a woman at the milk-bar across the road from the bus-stop — said she'd seen a car stop and pick Linda up. Wasn't she able to give you a description of the man or the car?"

The inspector laughed shortly. "Oh, yes. Miss Maxwell. She knew Linda Benmore by sight and when Mrs Benmore started making enquiries about Linda she went to the milk-bar. Miss Maxwell told her a man in a car had picked Linda up. But Miss Maxwell, apart from being emphatic that the child picked up was Linda, could tell us very little — simply, of course, because there was nothing in the incident to arouse her interest. Which confirms your feeling that Linda was perfectly willing and happy to ride with the man who offered the lift."

Sergeant Connor added, "Miss Maxwell, we gather, doesn't like policemen, on principle. But she likes kids and would have told us if she'd known anything. She did, oddly enough, confirm your opinion that the car was either a Holden or a Falcon — though I felt she might be naming the only two makes of cars she knows. She also said it was white or cream. But on second thoughts, it might have been light blue, or green."

"She and I make two very reliable witnesses," Philip said bitterly.

The policemen moved toward the door. "There may have been other witnesses, Mr Blair. Don't worry about it. You've been helpful."

★ ★ ★

It was a long night that brought Philip little sleep as he went over and over the few seconds when a sighted man could have identified a killer — might well have stopped the crime from ever happening, because these deranged people usually struck on a random impulse, and this one certainly wouldn't have risked picking up the child had he not known her companion couldn't identify him.

It had still been a risk, of course: Linda might very well have addressed him by name.

Philip thought about that. Could it be that, although the man was familiar to Linda, she didn't know his name? You could pass the time of day with the postman, the bus-driver, the man in the butcher's shop, every day of the week for years, and not know their names. Or it might be someone who usually waited for the bus at the same stop as Linda.

It was a long day.

He found the way to the bus-stop without much bother, but the too-early-for-the-bus silence was chilling. When the regulars did come, they talked about Linda. Some of them, Philip gathered, hadn't even known her name, but the bus-stop number had been made public in the hope of finding witnesses, and the bus-passengers were a little chagrined they could offer no help. Only Mr Giordano, when he came accompanied by his cigar, spoke to Philip.

"You were the man here when that rat picked Linda up, weren't you, mister?"

"Yes," Philip said.

Mr Giordano grunted. "Got a little girl myself." Philip heard the grimness in the big Italian's voice. Presently Mr Giordano added, "Feel a bit sick, don't you, mister? Don't fret. Dirty rat wouldn't 'a done it only he knew you couldn't see him. Ours," he tacked on as a bus pulled in to the kerb.

He sat beside Philip on the way in

toward the city centre.

"She went with him happy-like?" he asked after a while.

"Yes," Philip said. "He called her by name. He just pulled up and opened the door and offered a lift and she accepted. That's when she told me to ask you about the bus."

Mr Giordano nodded ponderously. "She and I catch this bus five years. Nice little girl. Real nice. She knew him, you know, mister. How do I know? The first six months we get this same bus, she never talk to me, not how much I try. That little girl, she never went with no man she didn't know. Parents taught her good."

Philip nodded slowly. "I'm sure you're right. From the way she spoke, I was sure she knew him. Mr Giordano, how many people regularly wait at that bus-stop?"

"Two school-boys, a young lady, Tom Fielding who works in an office, Mrs Stone who works in a dress-shop, Linda and me. Sometimes a lady or two going shopping early."

"No other man?"

31

"Oh, a few times, old Mr Weller. He's eighty."

"This Tom someone: was he on the bus yesterday?"

"Sure."

"You're quite certain?"

"Sure. I was going to ask him to tell you your stop, but he took a seat right at the other end of the bus, so I ask that lady instead. That's how I'm sure. Anyway, Tom's okay."

★ ★ ★

Robert Henderson was waiting for him when the bus pulled up at the school stop.

"Hey," he said lightly, "you don't look as if you've had any sleep since I saw you two days ago."

He frowned, and added, "Phil, you're not letting Taylor bug you, are you? Or the job generally?"

Philip shook his head. "No. Oh, Taylor bugs me, all right. Sometimes I'd like to kick him into the middle of next week."

"I can imagine. I've had this hearing

problem all my life." Henderson touched the plug in his right ear. "When I was at school, a kid in the sixth grade thought it was very funny to pinch the battery so I couldn't hear in class. But Phil, it's early days yet, and you've won nearly all the kids to your side. They've stopped looking at you like the eighth wonder of the world and have started noticing you're a good teacher."

"Which is more than can be said for our admiring principal, who is confidently waiting for me to flop so he can say, 'I told you so' to the board."

"Disappoint him."

"I intend to." He sighed. "It's not the job, Rob." He explained about Linda Benmore as they went into the staff-room.

Robert whistled. "You attract trouble like corned-beef attracts blow-flies, don't you?"

Philip pulled a face. "Ever thought of writing poetry? You have such a picturesque turn of phrase. Incidentally, you seem to have made a quick recovery. Weren't you on sick-leave yesterday? Or was it just a hang-over from too much youthful exuberance the night before?"

"Don't be so nasty. I had to take to my bed yesterday — blasted asthma playing up a bit."

One of the other teachers said, "Must have been a sudden attack. I phoned your flat at a quarter to eight to ask you to bring back that book, and your brother answered and said you'd left early for work. Did the asthma just come on as you were driving in?"

Another staff member looked up from his paper. "Left for work by a quarter to eight? I thought the boss said you phoned him about six-thirty to tell him you weren't coming in."

Robert raised an eyebrow. "And to think no one ever told me the Spanish Inquisition had been re-convened."

There was an edge of irritation under the banter. "Oh, all right, if I must give an account of myself. Ken wasn't up when I left — he's the one who was suffering an overdose of youthful exuberance — and he just assumed I'd gone to work. In fact, I wanted to make sure Philip had made it to the bus-stop safely, so although I was feeling pretty lousy I drove around to check. He was there all right, so I went home."

He looked at Philip. "Sorry, old man. I didn't mean to let you know that Big Brother was watching you."

But there was only sharp attention in Philip's face. "Then you'd have driven past about the time Linda Benmore was picked up."

"Well, *I* didn't see anything."

"But think, Robert! Are you sure?"

"Of course I'm damned well sure! The child wasn't there. You were alone at the bus-stop. I just kept driving."

There was a little silence. "Damn and damn," Philip said tiredly. "How lucky can the swine be?"

★ ★ ★

Philip went through the day with his mind only half on his work. The Grade Twelve boys seemed aware of it and were restless. Shortly after the start of the class Philip heard carefully quiet footsteps moving toward the door.

Jolted back to attention by the memory of the multiplicity of tricks employed by

35

James Taylor to show how contemptuously Philip's authority could be flouted — including one Taylor-organized stealthy mass walk-out that left Philip with an empty class-room — Philip said: "Who is walking about, please?"

"Taylor," a voice said coolly. "Just going for a drink of water."

"My classes certainly are not conducted with military discipline. But people do not wander in and out without explanation. And they address me as 'sir'. Sit down."

"I raised my hand to ask permission, but you didn't appear to notice. Sir."

There was a little silence. Then Philip said quietly, "Taylor, I credit you with enough intelligence to know that that is a singularly inane remark. Now I suggest it's time we brought this whole thing out into the open. You've set out to obstruct me from the beginning. Why?"

Taylor didn't answer.

"How old are you? Seventeen?"

"Yes," Taylor admitted.

"Right. Then you're a man, not the child you've been behaving as. So, man to man, what have you against me?"

Taylor hesitated, and when he spoke his voice was a sneer. "My parents — all our parents — have to pay thumping big fees to send us to St Stephen's. We have every right to expect the best in teachers, not crocks who can't hold their own in State schools."

"You think I can't teach?"

"Of course you can't bloody well teach! And you know it. Just who you know on the Board I don't know, but you must have used some influence somewhere. The State Education Department wouldn't employ you, and neither they should. Okay, so being blinded was bad luck; but it was your bad luck. It shouldn't be ours, too. You can't earn your place in any school. You can't control a class you can't see, you can't set tests and you can't mark exam papers. Of course you can't bloody well teach!"

The class was dead still. Philip rubbed the back of his neck. "Uh-huh. Well, it's true that the State wasn't keen on the idea of me as a teacher, any more than you are. I didn't know anyone on the Board of this school when I applied for the job, and I was accepted on my past ability — with the proviso that I must prove myself in the job. I can't control a class, as you put it, if controlling means having to watch their every move and being able to hit them over the ear if they misbehave. I would have thought young men would be beyond that. And it's perfectly true I can't mark exam papers. I earn my keep by taking more classes than my fellow-teachers while they spend that extra time on the necessary paper-work."

He paused. "But I can teach, Mr Taylor. I can teach. And if you will sit down and shut up and listen for long enough, I'll show you that I can bloody well teach!"

He heard James Taylor walk back to his seat and he knew that at least he had gained the full attention of the class. Somewhere inside him he felt he had just won a small victory. Maybe he had begun to convince these boys that he *could* teach.

And maybe that was the beginning of convincing himself.

★ ★ ★

He took a taxi from the school to police headquarters and listened to the tapes of voices of men who liked to make obscene or threatening telephone calls, but none, at least to his ears, matched the voice of the man in the car.

"But it's very hard to be sure," he told Sergeant Connor when he had picked out three possible voices, "because the man who picked Linda up had a cold, or sounded as if he did. And there were so few words, and those few were so normal, that I have very little to go on."

He stood up to go. "If it's none of my business, Sergeant, just tell me so. But — you have the post-mortem results?"

"Yes. There's no reason why you shouldn't know them, Mr Blair. The child was killed by several blows about the head with a heavy piece of timber which was left beside the body — no finger-prints on it, of course. The initial blow almost certainly caused unconsciousness. Although the body was only partly clothed and the rest of the clothing left scattered beside it, she had not been sexually assaulted. Evidently her attacker was disturbed and panicked."

"Do you think the workmen who found the body disturbed him?"

"No. The child had been dead for some hours when they arrived in the area. It seems the man must have driven directly there after picking her up, and killed her. We've put out an appeal to the public for anyone who was in the area of that side-road yesterday morning to come forward. Someone may have seen something."

"Is the road used much?"

"Too much, and too little," the sergeant said drily. "Too little to have much hope anyone saw anything of consequence. Too much to let us pick up significant tyre tracks. And the particular spot where the body was found is grassy: no foot-prints that mean anything."

"It sounds," Philip said harshly, "as though he thought of everything."

"Either that, or he was lucky. It's often the toughest kind of murder to crack — the one where some nut who otherwise looks perfectly human just picks out a victim at random, kills, and walks away."

Philip's hands clenched. "You mean

you have very little chance of catching him."

The sergeant laughed mirthlessly. "We've barely started, Mr Blair. We're an awfully long way from giving up. In fact, you know, we never do give up. Not in ten years nor in twenty. Every man on this job is as anxious to get this man as you are. Every member of the public wants him. This fellow has no friends."

They sent Philip home in a police car. Listening to it pull away from the kerb outside his flat, he thought, as he had been thinking all day, of the car pulling away from him, taking a child to violent death. Holden or Falcon. He and the waitress at the milk-bar both said that. But how reliable was either guess? Just a guess.

Like him, the waitress hadn't taken much notice. He frowned reflectively.

She *had* noticed. Did that mean there had been something unusual, something out of the ordinary? Something unusual, or something — familiar?

★ ★ ★

It nagged him for a week. Finally, one afternoon when he got off the bus, he didn't cross at the pedestrian crossing but simply stood waiting until a footfall sounded on the footpath, and he asked, "Excuse me, I'm blind. I wonder would you walk with me to the milk-bar?"

"Certainly," a woman's voice answered. "It's only three doors along."

She put a hand lightly on his arm and walked beside him with a few casual words about the weather. Then: "Here we are. Turn hard left, step up eight inches — what's that in centimetres? — and you're there. Do you want to go to one of the tables, or a stool at the milk-bar, or do you just want something at the counter?"

"If you'd be so kind as to direct me to the counter."

The woman did so, brushed aside his thanks and left.

Another woman's voice — quite different, with a slightly nasal, harsh accent — said, "Yes, please?" with disinterest.

"May I speak to Miss Maxwell for a moment?"

A second of silence while, Philip knew, the woman looked him over curiously.

"Are you Miss Maxwell?" he asked.

"Who wants to know?"

"My name's Philip Blair."

"Cop or newspaper reporter?"

"Neither. I'm a school-teacher. But I'm the man who was at the bus-stop on Tuesday morning when Linda Benmore was abducted. I'm surprised you don't recognize me. After all, it was you who described me to the police."

"Oh, you're the bloke?" Her tone was interested now. "Yes, I suppose you are. But it was clear across the street from here and I never took much notice — why should I? I mean, I was busy about me work, and you look for yourself — it's a wide street: when you're not taking any special notice, how much do you think *you'd* notice a bloke at the bus-stop?"

"I wouldn't notice him at all. I'm blind."

The woman looked him over intently, prominent blue eyes frankly curious. They were shrewd eyes that had had nearly forty years of experience at weighing up the human race — with an especially keen interest, over the past twenty-five years, in weighing up the male half of it.

She saw now a man a couple of years past thirty, tallish and a bit too thin, but with a whipcord-toughness about him. She studied the sensitive face with the wide mouth set at a slightly sardonic angle that gave him a cynical look.

Philip said pleasantly, "Miss Maxwell, it seems you and I are the only witnesses. I can give so little information. I wondered whether, if we talked about it together, we might come up with something we've forgotten."

She still didn't answer, and he said, "I only met Linda for the first time that morning, but I liked her. The man who did this should be caught in case he kills again. The police told me you like children."

"Cops! I shouldn't have thought they'd notice," she said contemptuously. "Come over to a table where we can talk a bit."

"I don't want to interrupt your work — "

"That's all right," she assured him with

alacrity. "I'll just tell the boss."

She was back after a quick murmur of voices, took his arm and steered him to a table. She settled her medium-height, slightly too plump figure opposite him, tossed her long wavy black hair back and said expectantly, "What do you want to know?"

"Will you think back, and try to tell me exactly what you saw on Tuesday morning?"

She sighed. "What I keep telling everybody. I seen the kid at the stop, and a car stopped and she got in. That's all. I just never took no notice. Why should I? I was busy with me work."

"But although you were busy you *did* notice. There must have been a reason."

She shook her head doubtfully, and he cut in before she could speak, "I'll tell you exactly what happened as I know it."

When he'd finished, he said, "Now, if you'll just think back. Did you see me arrive at the bus-stop?"

"No. I seen Linda there when I came into the shop — I come in the back

45

way. She's — she was always there early. I knew her name from coming in here — her mother often used to tell her to get something from here on her way home from school. We have stuff like sausage, and fish and chips, and bread and bottles of milk and all that, and Linda's been coming in for years. Nice kid, quiet, no cheek like some."

She stopped and asked curiously, "You want to know all the things I did in the shop?"

"Yes, please, Miss Maxwell. What you did and what you saw."

"Okay. Name's Irene, by the way — makes me feel more comfortable. Well, I got a bundle of old newspapers from the back and put 'em on the counter for wrapping fish and chips and things. Oh, we wrap 'em in proper white paper first," she added hastily. "But a few layers of newspaper keeps 'em hot. Well, when I came back in the shop, you were at the bus-stop and I thought: hello, here's someone new. So I took notice of you, and that's how I could describe you to the police."

So, Philip thought with a twist of

disappointment, it was only the sight of a strange man at the bus-stop that made her notice anything.

Irene Maxwell rested her chin thoughtfully on her hands. "Let's see, now, what did I do then? Piled the newspapers on the counter, I suppose. We only use the morning papers because they've got them big sheets. Then we cut 'em down the fold by sort of tearing 'em with the back of a knife, and just use the single sheets. So that's what I'd be doing — cutting the sheets. We hadn't any customers; we'd only just opened. I just glanced up, and there was a car stopped at the bus-stop."

"Right," Philip said encouragingly as she paused. "Now, shut your eyes and try to *see* it happen. And tell me what you see."

She obediently closed her eyes.

"The car stopped, and the driver was leaning across, away from me, as if he was opening the door. Linda was standing beside you, looking up at you as if she was talking to you, and I remember wondering if you were her father — I don't know him. And then she got into

47

the car and it drove away."

"Uh-huh. And when the man sat up straight again, to drive away, did you see his face?"

"Never took any notice."

"But he'd have turned his head this way to look for traffic before he pulled out from the kerb."

There was a little silence, and Philip felt himself tense sharply. "There was something — " Irene stopped with a puzzled frown.

"No," she decided. "I just never took any notice."

"But you think there was something — what? Familiar about this man? You felt you'd seen him somewhere before?"

"No. Just for a minute something went through me mind but I don't know what it was — nothing important. Anyway, it's gone."

"Try to think," he urged. "Try closing your eyes again, trying to recall the scene exactly."

In a few moments she said, "No. I don't remember anything."

"There was something unusual, wasn't there? Something about the man — or

48

the car. Or maybe something the man did, or something in the way Linda acted."

"No, there wasn't nothing like that. If there had been," Irene said reasonably, "I'd have remembered, wouldn't I?"

Philip hit the table a little bump with his fist. "But that's just it! You *do* remember. Therefore there must have been something unusual about the thing."

He hitched his chair closer to the table, eagerly. "Irene, don't you see? Nine hundred and ninety-nine times in a thousand you wouldn't notice a child at a bus-stop get into a car. So why did you notice this?"

Irene shrugged. "Because it made me think of that other little girl, I suppose."

Philip sat bolt upright. "What other little girl?"

"Oh, that one a couple of weeks ago. You know — it was in all the papers."

"I don't," Philip said drily, "read the papers."

"Oh. Oh, gee, I'm sorry — I didn't mean — "

He made a quick gesture with his hand

49

as if brushing something aside. "It's all right. But you'll have to tell me about it. What happened to the other little girl?"

"Well, this kid started off for school one morning and just never came home. The papers were full of it next day. Seems she wasn't the sort of kid that went missing. I mean, some do, and some don't. Well, there was a big search, police and everything, and the public asked to co-operate — you know the sort of thing. Day after she went missing, someone found her school-bag and hat on the bank of the river, and skin-divers found her body."

"Was it a sex attack?"

"No. Oh, no, nothing like that. Just played hookey from school and went fishing in the river in a quiet spot. There was a fishing-line still in the water. Must've over-balanced and fell in."

Philip sat blankly. "Then why," he asked politely after a moment, "did that come to mind when you saw Linda get into the car? Did the other little girl come from Walton Hill, too?"

"Oh, no. Right over Indooroopilly way somewhere, I think. They were about the

50 May/96

same age, though."

"But," Philip persisted, "there must have been more to it than that — something to make you connect them."

Irene shook her head. "Maybe. I don't know. You see, as I was spreading the old newspapers on the counter I seen the bit about the other little girl being drowned, and I'd just been reading it again when I looked up and seen Linda getting into the car, and it just made me think: 'Just like that other little girl.' That's all. You know the way a thing'll come into your mind sudden-like."

"Yes. But there's usually a reason."

Irene sighed. "Well, I suppose it was because they thought at first the other little girl might have been ab — ab — kidnapped, and I seen Linda getting into this car."

Philip snapped with an irritability born of disappointment: "I really can't see much connection between an accidental drowning in one suburb and an abduction and sex murder in another."

Irene flushed slightly. "You don't know it *was* a sex murder, do you, Mr Smart

Blair? Maybe someone just wanted it to look that way."

"What do you mean?" he demanded.

"Just that we don't *know* why Linda was killed, do we? We *think* we know, that's all. Might be right, might be wrong. You think I'm dumb. All right, so I don't know anything. I'm just telling you you don't know all the answers, either."

There was a pause. Philip nodded. "You're quite right, of course. I'm sorry I snapped at you. I wanted to find out that you knew something useful, that's all."

He asked her some more questions, about the car, about the man. Her answer remained the same: she didn't remember; she hadn't taken any particular notice. Finally he gave up, thanked her and asked her to call a taxi. Suddenly he felt he couldn't face that walk home. He felt overwhelmed by disappointment.

Irene Maxwell knew nothing of consequence.

3

BUT it nagged him.

Time after time he snapped awake during the night, and at disturbingly forceful intervals the next day fragments of what Irene Maxwell had said kept leaping into his head, almost audibly.

"You don't know it *was* a sex murder, do you, Mr Smart Blair?" "Just for a minute something went through me mind, but it's gone." "It made me think of that other little girl." That repeated itself, again and again. "It made me think of that other little girl."

When he'd finished his dinner the next evening he telephoned a policeman friend he hadn't spoken to for more than two years.

"Des? It's Philip Blair."

A second of silence, and then: "Philip? Philip! I don't believe it. I thought you'd dropped all your old friends for keeps."

The voice was slow and tinted with

laughter, and Philip smiled faintly at the memories.

"I know. I'm revoltingly anti-social. But just living is fairly complicated these days. The routine things don't seem to leave a lot of time for niceties."

"Sure, Phil, I know. Well, what can I do for you — or is that just my nasty suspicious mind and you only called because you've missed my sparkling company?"

Philip laughed. "Your nasty suspicious mind is bang-on. Look, Des, are you still a policeman?"

"Uh-huh. Sergeant, no less."

"Congratulations. I don't know whether what I'm asking is ethical — or even legal — "

"Marvellous! If no one broke laws, I'd be unemployed."

"Shut up and listen. You know about the little girl who was found murdered on Tuesday afternoon."

"I do." His tone was at once sober and attentive.

"Well — " Philip told him briefly of his own indirect connection and his conversation with Irene Maxwell.

"The thing is crazy, I'm sure, Des," he concluded, "but I wonder if you could find out about the little girl who was drowned — check whether it's certain it was an accident."

Des Maddock said slowly, "You think this waitress knows something more than she was telling?"

Philip sighed. "I don't know. I don't think she consciously knows anything. But there could be something in the back of her mind making her link the two girls."

"Okay, I'll check. It's a bit out of my line — I'm in traffic — but I can get the details."

He paused a moment. "It's bothering you, isn't it, Phil? Why?"

"Oh, it's just — just that the damned fellow picked the kid up from right beside me, knowing he was perfectly safe from me. Knowing he could look at me and say to himself: he's harmless."

Philip gave a quick hard laugh. "That wounds my ego. I don't want to see him get away with it. All right, so I *was* harmless and I've got to forget it, but I can't quite forget it until I'm sure Irene

Maxwell was just being what I presume is her usual gossipy self. I don't want to go running to the homicide fellows with a lot of hoo-hah that wastes their time. So if you could possibly be a good fellow and check that there's no possible connection between the two deaths — "

"Will do. No trouble. I know a couple of the chaps in homicide pretty well — tried to get into the branch myself, only the powers-that-be didn't recognize brilliant material when they saw it. But Phil," he added seriously, "the chances are about five hundred to one your waitress is purely romancing. We get 'em in droves in every case."

Philip smiled wryly. "I know. I hope there's absolutely nothing in it, believe me. I don't want to start playing detective, Des. I'm not exactly equipped for it, and these days my life is complicated enough. There's no room for any kind of extra involvements."

"Are you telling me that's why you broke off with Penny?"

"That is exactly why I broke off with Penny."

"I see. Well, I'll check, to set your

mind at rest, and I'll phone you back. What's your address and number?"

The same. I kept the flat. It was easier to adjust to familiar surroundings."

"I suppose it would be. I'll call you when I get the information."

Philip thanked him and hung up, then leaned back in the easy-chair beside the phone and found his face was damp with perspiration in the pleasantly-cool autumn evening.

Is that why you broke off with Penny?

He had tried — as he asked the operator on Information to get Des' number, as he waited while Des' phone rang — not to let himself feel any sense of shock, any emotion at all, if it were Penny's voice that answered.

He had cut himself off so completely from almost all the old associations that he simply didn't know whether Penny had married Des. He still didn't know. Not that it mattered. Not to him.

In that shattered world of blackness into which he'd been so violently plunged, he'd shut her out of his life.

It was queer, to think back — queer partly because it was all so distant, so unfamiliar now, like a story he'd heard about other people. Normally he never allowed himself to think back.

Those two years might have been two lifetimes. He'd been a teacher of history and English in a State high school, he'd been buying a neat, unpretentious house on a pleasant block of land.

And he'd been engaged to marry Penelope Cosgrove, a pharmaceutical chemist with shining copper-gold hair, a slightly snub nose with the faintest dusting of freckles, a generous mouth and green eyes always ready to laugh — a girl who wasn't exactly pretty but always left the impression that she was.

He took a long, slow breath. He hadn't let himself think about Penny for two years. Even now, he wouldn't have done it, except that speaking to Des had brought it back too forcefully to be ignored — that other world to which he had once belonged.

Once, he'd been afraid he might lose Penny to Des. Then, when he'd been blinded, he'd been grateful that Des was there in the background. It had meant he could slam the door on Penny and know she could turn to Des if she wanted to. He didn't have to worry about her.

Is that why you broke off with Penny? What was the use of trying to explain — to Des or to anyone — that suddenly all the others, all the people with sight, had become aliens. Strangers. Worse than strangers. Almost enemies, because they pitied you. And it was not in Philip Blair's nature to be pitied.

Certainly he had not turned Penny out of his life from any desire to shield her from the difficulties and frustrations of being a blind man's wife. Perhaps he had done it out of a desperate need to shield himself — from her pity, which would be worse than all the rest of the world's pity; from being a man dependent on his wife.

He let himself remember how he had told her, bluntly, without regard for how much he hurt her, perhaps even wanting to hurt her; told her that he was much too busy trying to rebuild his life to be able to find any room in it for her.

"And don't go around," he'd said savagely, "thinking you could help me. You couldn't. You'd only burden me. I'm

59

sorry. Everything's so totally different. I can't feel the same about you any more."

There had been a long, still silence. Then she had said very quietly, "I see."

And she had walked out of the room and he had never heard from her again. And that was as it should be.

★ ★ ★

On the Saturday evening Des Maddock phoned back.

"I got all the details of that drowning, Phil. I'm sorry to disappoint your sensation-hungry waitress friend, but at least I can set your mind at rest. Absolutely no suspicious circumstances. She was a school-girl named Shirley Philbrook, twelve years. Left home as usual to go to school, hue and cry raised when she didn't come home, and the mother found that she never went to school that day."

"The story was broadcast along with a description of the girl and the usual police fears for her safety. Usual public response: she'd been seen in Gympie, in

Sandgate; getting on to the pillion seat of a motorcycle ridden by a bearded youth, climbing into a white Falcon sedan, boarding the Sydney train at South Brisbane, and hitch-hiking on Ipswich Road.

"Then next day all the reports were proved false. Her small suitcase of school-books was found in long grass on the bank of the river in a secluded spot. A fishing line was still trailed in the water. Part of her lunch was still in an open greaseproof-paper parcel on the bank. The fish-hook was caught, entangled in some water-weed. Evidently Shirley must have been trying to free it when she overbalanced and fell into the river."

"I see," Philip said slowly. "There was no hint of foul play?"

"None. Death was due to drowning. There were no injuries and no sex assault."

"Couldn't she swim?"

"Yes," Des told him. "Tolerably well, apparently. But all manner of things could have happened — shock, the way the current caught her, perhaps she even got tangled in the weed where the fish-hook was caught. The skin-divers found the body about fifty yards downstream, presumably carried there by the current."

"Was there any explanation of why she should have played hookey and gone fishing? Had it happened before?"

He had a sharp recollection of Irene Maxwell's voice saying, "Seems she wasn't the sort of kid that went missing."

"No," Des said. "It baffled the mother, apparently. There was no father, incidentally — divorced, and hasn't been heard of in years. But the mother said she knew of no reason why the kid should play hookey, and no reason why she'd go fishing, since she'd never displayed any interest. The line was a new one — just hook, line, sinker line wrapped around an empty Coke bottle. Sort of thing a kid might buy with a bit of pocket-money, of course. The mother knew nothing about it."

So, Philip thought when he'd thanked Des and hung up, he could write the whole thing off. Irene Maxwell had been romancing over it.

But one thing kept surfacing in his

mind: Des saying, "She'd been seen in Gympie, in Sandgate, getting on to the pillion seat of a motorcycle, climbing into a white Falcon sedan, boarding the Sydney train, and hitch-hiking on Ipswich Road."

He himself had identified by sound the car which picked up Linda Benmore as probably Falcon or Holden. Irene Maxwell had said the same, and called it white or cream. True, she had also said it might have been green or blue.

He sighed. It was all nonsense. There was no connection.

As if on cue, the phone rang.

Irene Maxwell's voice said, "Is that Mr Philip Blair? I've remembered something about the little girl Benmore. Can you come over to the milk-bar? Not tonight — place is full and the boss'd have a fit. Tomorrow morning. I work tomorrow morning."

Philip said with a touch of irritability, "Why are you calling me? If you have any information, you should tell the police."

"Huh!" She sniffed scornfully. "I don't want no dealings with the coppers, thank you. Can you come to see me?"

Philip frowned. He wanted to say "No" and hang up. But there was something in Irene Maxwell's manner, something excited.

"I suppose it's a bit difficult," she said. "I'll come round to your place about twelve, if you like. I knock off then."

"All right," Philip said.

★ ★ ★

At a few minutes past midday she knocked on his door. Inside, as she put down her handbag and settled herself in an easy chair, she looked around with frank curiosity.

"You don't live here all by yourself?" she demanded.

"I do."

"Laws! How do you manage? I mean, you couldn't cook or anything, could you?"

"I can, actually. If it interests you, I have a cleaning-lady come once a week and I send out my laundry. Miss Maxwell, what — "

"Irene, love. I like it better. You know, your flat's tidier than mine!"

"It has to be tidy. Now — "

"Yes, I suppose it does, otherwise you wouldn't find things. 'Course, I've always heard that blind people sort of develop special instincts."

"They don't, and I have plenty of scars and bruises to prove it. Now will you please tell me what it is you've remembered — if anything."

"Huh! Lovely manners, haven't you? Well, all right." She chuckled comfortably. "Mine aren't so hot, either, I guess."

She leaned forward. "You think I'm stupid. Well, maybe and maybe not. But I wasn't being stupid when I said seeing Linda reminded me of the other little girl. I'd just been reading about it in the old newspaper, like I told you, and then I seen Linda getting into the car, and straightaway it clicked. But I couldn't think for the life of me why, afterwards. Then yesterday out of the blue it hit me.

"They went to the same school!" she said triumphantly, settling back to watch his reaction.

He looked puzzled. "But — they lived miles apart — almost on opposite sides of Brisbane. How do you know they went to the same school?"

"Same uniform. There was a picture of the other little girl in the paper. And that's what clicked when I seen Linda. Same school uniform."

"But Shirley Philbrook was accidentally drowned."

"How come you know her name?" Irene demanded suspiciously. "The other day, you'd never heard of her."

"I checked with a police officer who is a friend of mine. And you can be sure the police are confident there are no suspicious circumstances."

"Coppers! What would they know?"

"A good deal, usually."

"Huh! I could tell them a few things they *don't* know." She laughed, and there was a touch of excitement in the laugh.

He said sharply, "About Linda Benmore?"

"I never said that. About a lot of things. *And* much good it would do. I'm telling *you* about Linda Benmore and this Shirley Whosis, and how much notice are you taking? 'You can be sure the police are confident there are no suspicious circumstances,'" she mimicked.

He said wearily, "Irene, you're not really telling me anything. What if the two girls did go to school together? What does it signify? One is accidentally drowned, and the other falls victim to a maniac."

"Says you. But how do you know that, eh? No one saw the first kid fall in the river. Her mother reckoned she wouldn't have gone fishing and she wouldn't have played hookey from school in the first place. She wasn't known to have a fishing line. It *looks* as if she accidentally drowned. That's all we know."

"Parents," Philip said drily, "don't always know as much about their children as they imagine they do."

Irene chuckled. "You can say that again. But suppose this one was right? And take Linda. Victim of a sex-maniac? But the papers said 'No criminal assault'. So how do you know it was a maniac, eh? It looks like it, that's all."

She dropped her voice a little, conspiratorially.

"Two kids, same age, same school, die violent deaths a couple of weeks apart, and no hard-and-fast answers on either death. You ask your policeman pal about that, Mr Blair."

Philip sat silently for a moment, chin on his hands. "Very well," he said. "I'll bring it to the attention of the police."

"Good." She stood up and, hearing the movement, so did he.

She paused and looked at him. "Do you suppose," she asked, "there'll be some kind of reward offered — you know, for information leading to the arrest of whoever killed Linda Benmore?"

He stiffened. "Irene, do you know something? Something more than you've told me?"

She laughed, and the excitement was back in her voice. "'Course not. But my information might lead to an arrest, mightn't it?"

"I can't see how."

"They often do put up rewards for murders like this. Quite big rewards. I might get part of it."

"If you were entitled to any, which I very gravely doubt since your information isn't going to help much, it would be very little."

"Oh. You think so?"

"I'm sure of it." Bounty-hunting trollop, he thought savagely.

She sighed, and then gave another little laugh. "I'll have to look elsewhere for my fortune, then."

And with a cheerful goodbye, she was gone.

Philip stood for a long time, frowning in concentration.

There was nothing in what Irene Maxwell had said — nothing but the purest coincidence in the fact the two girls had attended the same school. Any idea of a link between the two had to be the product of wild imagination.

Somehow Irene, on seeing Linda in her school uniform just after looking at a photograph of Shirley Philbrook in hers, had recalled Shirley's death and — after hearing Linda had been murdered — turned loose an imagination eager for sensation.

And yet — Had it been his own imagination, or had there been something cunning, excited, too knowing, in Irene's attitude? She had been different from the first time he'd spoken to her. She could, he thought, have been drinking.

He shrugged. Her theory was nonsense. It was nothing more than the reaction of someone who found life duller than she would like it to be.

He went across the room and picked up his tape-recorder. He would phone the homicide branch tomorrow and tell them the two girls attended the same school; though he was sure they would know that already. But he had promised to do it.

Meanwhile, he could go back to his own battles with realities and leave sensation-seeking waitresses to their flights of morbid fancy. He had lessons to prepare for tomorrow's classes.

★ ★ ★

He was eating his breakfast the next morning while he listened to the radio news, not especially absorbed in the fact that large eggs were dearer by two cents a dozen.

Nor in the announcer's impersonal voice reading the next news item, until the name of his own suburb hit his ear.

70

"A young woman fell to her death from the fourth floor of a block of flats in George Road, Walton Hill, last night. She was Miss Irene Maxwell, thirty-eight, who lived alone in a small flat on the top floor of the building. Police said Miss Maxwell had apparently leaned over the window-sill to hang a dress to dry outside the window on a hook she had fastened to the window-frame for the purpose. She apparently lost her balance and fell to a concrete path below.

"In Rockhampton last night, thieves broke into a sports store owned — "

Philip switched off the set and sat in stunned stillness.

4

IRENE MAXWELL. The only person to see the man who picked up Linda Benmore.

Irene laughing and a little excited, asking if he thought she might get reward money for her information — and, when he said no, saying she would have to look elsewhere for her fortune. He'd thought nothing of that remark at the time, but the thought of it now invaded with a force that shut everything else out.

His mind flicked back to the afternoon in the milk-bar when he'd talked to Irene. He remembered asking if she'd seen the man's face and she'd said she'd taken no notice. And he recalled saying: "But he'd have turned his head this way, to look for traffic before he pulled out from the kerb."

And Irene had been silent for a moment and then had said slowly, "There was something — "

She had stopped and presently said,

"Just for a minute something went through me mind. But I don't know what it was. Anyway, it's gone."

He believed she was being honest, then, but yesterday there had been something sly, knowing, about her.

Had she remembered something about the driver of the car? Had she tried that most sublimely idiotic of ugly ways of making money: had she tried to blackmail a murderer?

A murderer had so little to lose by a second murder. Or a third. Irene had been so insistent there was a link between Linda's murder and Shirley Philbrook's apparently accidental death. She had advanced the theory that the connection was the fact that the girls attended the same school. But was even Irene's imagination as wild as that?

Philip picked up the telephone. The voice in the homicide branch told him Inspector Batlow wasn't in the office yet; may he take a message?

Philip told him of his conversation with Irene Maxwell, and was asked to come in to headquarters after work.

A police car picked him up at the

school and the cheerful constable who drove it guided him to Inspector Batlow's office.

Philip reported his conversation with Irene Maxwell as accurately as he could. When he had finished, Inspector Batlow said:

"You say Miss Maxwell seemed excited — until you told her there was very little prospect her information would result in her being paid reward money, no doubt?"

Philip shook his head. "It didn't discourage her at all. She just said she'd have to look elsewhere for her fortune. She denied it, but I felt she'd remembered more than she'd admit. That's why I wonder now if she had ideas of trying her hand at blackmail."

Batlow raised an eyebrow. "Are you suggesting, Mr Blair, that Miss Maxwell's death was not an accident?"

Philip made an impatient movement. "Inspector, aren't there too many coincidences? Irene Maxwell was the only person to see the man who picked up Linda Benmore. She has insisted that there was a connection

74

between Linda and Shirley Philbrook. Linda and Shirley attended the same school. Both are dead — and both, as Irene pointed out, in circumstances that may be deceptive. And now Irene Maxwell herself is dead — and again the cause of death may not be what it seems."

"We have absolutely no evidence to suggest that either Irene Maxwell or Shirley Philbrook died by foul play, Mr Blair. We will, of course, continue to make the fullest investigations into Miss Maxwell's death. I might point out, of course, that Miss Maxwell's name was never made public as a witness to the abduction of Linda Benmore."

"That wouldn't matter if she tried blackmail; she'd identify herself."

The inspector stood up. "That's true. I assure you we haven't overlooked the possibility of violence. Now, if you'll just go with the sergeant he'll arrange transport home for you. And thank you for your help, Mr Blair."

Class dismissed, Philip thought wryly; are they as disbelieving as they seem?

★ ★ ★

The man sat quietly in his car, hat at a nonchalant angle, dark glasses hiding the fact that his eyes were not on the afternoon paper he held so casually. He might have been a father waiting to pick up his children as the youngsters came out in chattering groups through the school gates. No one gave him a second glance.

There was no one to notice that the eyes behind the dark glasses watched only the girls — watched with an absorbed, calculating intentness. There was no one to notice that he waited a little while after they were all gone, as if he felt there might be a straggler or two.

Then, as no one else came out through the gates, he put down the newspaper and drove away. His movements were all easy, deliberate. He gave no sign of disappointment or irritation, except for a small frown. His attitude suggested that he was a patient man who would be prepared to wait and wait again.

★ ★ ★

Philip phoned Des Maddock, who cheerfully promised to try to find out what police thinking on Irene Maxwell's death really was.

Next evening he rang Philip's doorbell. "Hope you don't mind the personal call," he said half-apologetically. I just thought — well, it's a long time."

Philip smiled. "Glad to have you come. I'm much too much a hermit, I know. I'm just about to make coffee — have some? After all, I'm using you, so you may as well get *something* in return. Or would you rather a drink?"

Des grinned. "Can a duck swim! Whisky, if you have it." He hesitated. "Ah — shall I get it?"

Philip shook his head. "Take a pew and watch how good I am at my housekeeping."

He poured a drink and handed it to Des, who took it and wandered around the livingroom while Philip made coffee for himself.

"The way you do things is fantastic," Des declared as they both sat down.

"Mmm. I wish I could be sure that would apply to my job."

"Problems?"

Philip shrugged. "Inevitably. There always are, whether you're sighted or not. What have you got for me?"

"Well, I've checked up on the old grapevine. The inspector wasn't just putting you off, old man. They're really quite satisfied your waitress friend died by misadventure — mainly because there's no reason to suppose otherwise."

"But damn it, Des, it's too — *neat*. I mean, she was the only person who saw the murderer of Linda Benmore. Suddenly she dies in a most peculiar way."

"Peculiar, yes," Des admitted, "but not entirely surprising. Seems her friends knew about her habit of hanging her milk-bar uniforms outside the window at night to dry. A couple of her girl-friends told the homicide boys that they'd often kidded her she'd fall out of the window one day. Actually, of course, it was a safe enough practice under normal circumstances. This time something went wrong. The dress was hanging askew on its coat-hanger. Evidently your friend Irene must have tried to straighten it, or maybe thought it was coming off the hanger and was going to fall. She must have made a grab for it, and leaned too far out."

"Did anyone outside see her fall?"

"No. Several people heard the thud as her body hit the concrete, but no one immediately investigated, not thinking of a fall. She was found by a neighbour who was out walking his dog. The doctor said she'd been dead about half an hour, and that tied in with the time people had heard the thud. There were multiple injuries. Death would have been instantaneous."

"No one heard a scream — any kind of a cry?"

"No." Des paused and then said gently, "Phil, there's just nothing to suggest foul play. No one was seen with Irene Maxwell that evening. No strangers were seen to enter or leave the flats. There were no fresh unaccountable fingerprints in the flat. There was not the slightest indication of a struggle."

"So the inspector wasn't just brushing me off as an interfering civilian? They really believe it was an accident? And

Shirley Philbrook's death was an accident?"

"They really believe both were accidents. Of the three deaths, there is one murder, and one murder only: Linda Benmore. If it's of any comfort to you, the boys are still interested in Miss Maxwell's death, because of the fact that she did see the man who picked Linda up. But her name was never made public — just reported as 'a witness reported having seen, etc.' And it was abundantly clear from all the reports that she couldn't give any kind of description."

Philip said slowly, "But just suppose she did in fact know, or remember, who the man in the car was? Suppose she tried blackmail?"

"After all this time? I mean to say, it's more than a week. If she knew something, surely she'd have acted sooner."

"Possibly. Maybe she did, and the murderer had to wait a favourable opportunity."

Des laughed. "Man, if I were in his shoes and a smart waitress was threatening me, I'd have *made* an opportunity. But seriously, Phil, if Irene Maxwell knew something, why didn't she say so at once? Our chaps never doubted at the time that she hadn't a clue what the man looked like or what make of car he drove — even its colour. I seem to remember you yourself felt she hadn't a clue the first time you saw her, and was only being self-important the second time."

Philip sighed. "Yes, I know. I suppose I'm barking up a tree that isn't even there. I just can't forget the thing, that's all. I wish I could."

★ ★ ★

He made an appointment to see Inspector Batlow and took a taxi from the school. After all, he told himself doggedly, they'll hardly throw me into prison; out on the street, possibly.

The inspector was guardedly cordial in his greeting, and he listened with the air of a man resolved to be polite as long as possible while Philip talked again of Irene's changed attitude of secretive excitement.

"It was not my imagination," Philip said. "The more I think of it, the surer I am that she had remembered something. How important it was I can't know, but whatever it was it strengthened her conviction that Linda's death and Shirley's were connected. Because her better self didn't want a child-killer to go free, she scattered suggestions. But because the greedy remainder of her saw a chance to make money, she wasn't going to come clean with any facts. Surely her death at least suggests she was too near the truth for someone's comfort."

Inspector Batlow eyed him coldly. "Mr Blair, do you imagine for one moment that we have been blind to the possible implications of Irene Maxwell's death? Do you think we would fail to check it out with every possible care? Do you think we're so damned stupid?"

"No," Philip admitted, "I don't."

"Thank you, Mr Blair. I could point out that at the time you attached no importance to Miss Maxwell's talk. The drama of her death, perhaps, has put things out of perspective for you. If there was one shred of evidence of foul play, we would not abandon investigations. Indeed, we haven't abandoned them. But there is nothing — and I mean nothing — to suggest that Miss Maxwell was not alone in the flat when she fell. She was quite a big woman, and strong. If anyone had tried to push her from a window she would have fought or at least screamed. There was no sign of a struggle and no scream was heard — and it seems certain it would have been heard.

"On the other hand, people who lean too far out of fourth floor windows are a bad insurance risk. As far as Shirley Philbrook is concerned, she was drowned in a simple accident. There is not and never has been anything to suggest any possible alternative. And there is no discernable link between her and Linda Benmore."

"Beyond attending the same school," Philip reminded him.

"Linda Benmore and Shirley Philbrook didn't attend the same school and never had."

Philip sat for some bewildered seconds. "But — why would Irene tell me that if it weren't true?"

Batlow shrugged. "She may have been trying to make herself more important to the case than in fact she was. It happens very often, especially with people who are a bit lonely."

He smiled. "Or she may have been using it as an excuse to see more of you. After all, Mr Blair, I should imagine women would regard you as an attractive man. Or, she may have genuinely believed what she said — why, I wouldn't know. We took the trouble, after you told us what Miss Maxwell had said, to check whether in fact the girls did know each other, or attend the same school. They didn't."

"I see." Philip stood up slowly. "I'm sorry, Inspector, to have taken up your time."

"Mr Blair," Batlow said seriously, "this thing especially plagues you. Can you tell me why? I´ mean, any man would be distressed at the thought that a little girl had been taken from right beside him, and murdered. But it means even more than that to you, doesn't it?"

Philip had turned toward where he knew the door to be. He turned back at the interest in the inspector's voice.

"Believe me, Inspector," he said very

quietly, "there's nothing I'd like better than to be able to go home and forget it. I've enough problems of my own. But I can't forget it. For two reasons.

"The first is that about two years ago I was attacked by three young men I'd never seen, in a busy city street, bashed and robbed of my wallet containing thirty dollars. Probably they mistook me for someone they knew would be carrying a lot of money. I regained consciousness a couple of hours later in hospital with only two things wrong with me: I had a headache, and I had permanently lost my sight."

His voice was coolly unemotional.

"My life had been unremarkable enough, but I liked it the way it was. The men who smashed it were never caught. There were plenty of bystanders, but they didn't try to help me because they didn't want to get involved in anything so nasty."

His voice was still steady, but a vein stood out on his temple. "I don't know any of them, but sometimes I hate them. I don't like getting involved in other people's business or in their problems, either. But I don't like violence and I don't like people who commit violent crimes to get away with them."

Batlow's grey eyes watched him thoughtfully for a moment. "I see. And the second reason?"

"He picked up the child from beside me because he knew I wouldn't identify him." Philip's voice rang hard as shod hooves on granite. "I don't like to feel helpless. I'm not that kind of man."

He moved toward the door. "Inspector, do you have any objections if I — well, to make it sound fearfully self-opinionated — make my own enquiries? I mean, ask questions of people to follow an idea?"

Batlow's eyes narrowed. "Do you have an idea?"

Philip shook his head. "No. But — you see, though my common sense tells me Irene Maxwell didn't know anything and made all the wrong guesses, something in me can't be sure."

He jammed his fists quickly into his trouser-pockets. "I've got to be *sure*. Sure to the level the law calls 'beyond reasonable doubt', I suppose. I know you're sure now, but I'm not, entirely. I've no idea right now what I can do, or what questions I can ask of whom. But if I do think of anything, do you have any objection if I follow it up privately?"

The inspector smiled. "None at all, Mr Blair."

5

PHILIP had just gone through the routine of washing-up his dinner dishes with the meticulous, measured movements that were essential, when someone knocked on his door.

He crossed the room with the confident stride born of deep familiarity with the precise position of every piece of furniture, opened the door wide and then stood frozen in pure shock.

He knew, as well as if he could see, who was standing there.

Her perfume, he decided, told him: a wisp of an almost-forgotten fragrance. And maybe some kind of instinct which, regardless of his changed feelings, would always enable him to know her, even in the dark.

A girl he would always see in his mind as he saw her last: a slim girl of twenty-two with copper-gold hair, a slightly snub nose with the faintest dusting of freckles, and a wide mouth.

A girl dressed in a shade of green that matched her eyes.

He knew before she could speak, though she was careful not to cheat with him, and spoke instantly.

"Hello, Philip. It's Penny. Penny Cosgrove."

He nodded. "Yes. Odd, that. I knew."

"Will you let me in?" she asked easily, and he knew by her voice that she was smiling.

He stepped back quickly, holding the door open. "Of course. Forgive my manners. I — you gave me something of a jolt. I never expected to meet you again."

"And hoped you never would." She said it lightly, and added at once, before he could feel any need to answer, "Des sent me. You can tell me to clear out and leave you in peace if you want to. But two years is a long time, Philip. I don't think I should be a disturbing element in your life."

He frowned in concentration, trying to keep his mind fully on the present, safely away from remembering. "Des sent you?"

"He said he thought you were about to go into business as a private detective — unpaid, of course. He thought you might find the loan of a pair of eyes useful."

She said it casually, matter-of-factly. "So I'm here as a pair of hired eyes only, to be accepted or rejected as such, and no ill feeling."

There was a little silence. Then Philip nodded. "Thank you, Penny. Des is perfectly right. I could use the loan of a pair of eyes. Unpaid, of course."

She laughed, and the laugh was as familiar as the perfume, though he would have thought he'd forgotten it. And suddenly there was no tension between them.

"First," he said, "you'd better sit down if you're going to listen to my version of the story. That arm-chair by the radio is probably the most comfortable."

"Fine," she said. "Would you mind putting the light on so I can find it?"

He felt himself flush. "Sorry. I do forget. Just a second."

He stepped back to the door and she heard his hand slide across the wall, feeling, before the light clicked on.

"How's that? Is it working?"

"Bright and clear," she told him.

She let her eyes run over his too-thin face with its darkly sardonic look, and she was momentarily glad he couldn't see her own face.

"You don't have many visitors, do you?"

He raised his eyebrows. "What makes you so sure I'm unpopular?"

"You had to feel for the switch. When you opened the door for me all your movements were clear-cut and confident, but you didn't quite know where the light-switch was."

"Observant as ever," he said drily. "I never could hide much from you."

"And I don't think," she went on as if he hadn't spoken, "that you're unpopular. I think you're shutting people out. It's not right, you know."

He made a non-committal noise and sat down.

"Before I begin to talk about this idea of mine, there's one thing you'd better understand — in fact, I imagine you know it already. Everyone thinks I'm some kind of kook, wanting to stay

91

with this thing. They think — well, they think: 'Poor fellow, it gives him a feeling of being important; psychologically that's very good for him; let's humour him.'"

Penny didn't answer.

"Well?" he demanded, anger flaring suddenly in his voice. "Isn't that more or less what Des told you?"

"More or less," she agreed quietly.

"And you're here in the same frame of mind? Oh, it doesn't follow that I won't take up your offer of help. But at least let's get off on an honest footing."

For a moment she didn't answer. Then she said slowly, "Philip, so often when a person loses a physical faculty, people want to be kind, but they're embarrassed because they can't know what life must be really like for the deprived person, and so they feel awkward — cut off. I think Des is a little like that. He could help you much more than I could, but he feels uncomfortable and not able to be natural with you. That's why he sent me."

A husbandly gesture, Philip thought. He said, "And you?"

Again he knew by her voice that she

smiled. "I didn't know how I'd feel. As helpless as Des or anyone else to really understand what life is like for you, certainly. But I can be natural and at ease with you. I didn't know how it would be, but that's how it is. As for whether you're a kook for following up an idea the police think is quite pointless — well, you may not be a detective, but I know perfectly well that if you're not satisfied that this affair is as straightforward as it seems, then you've a darned good reason for thinking so. So — if you believe an apparent accident was murder, I think there's got to be a chance it was. You're probably wrong. But you may be right, and I don't like murder, so let's get to work. Put me in the picture."

He smiled, and she marvelled as she always had at the way it lit and transformed his face.

He leaned back and relaxed. "Fair enough. But I can't say I *believe* an apparent accident was murder; I'm not at all satisfied it wasn't, that's all. And when I have put you in the picture, if you decide with the others that I'm trying to be important about nothing, will you say so?"

"With devastating rudeness," she said drily.

There was a small stillness. "Which, if I can hand it out, I should be able to take?" Philip suggested.

"That was a long time ago," she said quickly. "Too long to matter now."

"Perhaps. I wonder why you came here tonight? Really why? After the things I said to you — Did you come because you're sorry for me?"

"I came because Des asked me to come and seemed to think it was important. I never would have, otherwise," she said candidly.

He nodded. "Fair enough." He added casually, "Do you see much of Des these days?"

"We keep in touch occasionally." Her answer was as careless as his question. He couldn't know whether the casualness was as contrived.

"I haven't kept in touch," he admitted. "Haven't spoken to Des since I left hospital, till this business. I wanted to know what the police really thought, so

94

I asked Des to find out for me. It's not very attractive, is it, to simply use one's friends?"

She smiled. "I didn't get the impression Des minded."

"I always thought you and Des — "

"No." The word was quietly spoken, but it cut into his remark with an edged finality.

"Sorry. It's none of my business. It's just that — well, Des is a pretty personable sort of fellow. It was natural enough to think you and he — "

Penny smiled faintly. "Yes. But no."

"He seems — " Philip frowned. "Oh, I don't know. Not quite the same old Des."

Penny said briefly, "He's still a policeman, still a bachelor, still six-feet-one — whatever that is in centimetres — still weighing what he did two years ago, still would be insufferably handsome if he wore a beard. He still plays squash and spends most of his spare time and money on those radio-controlled model aeroplanes he was always so keen on. But he's thirty-five instead of thirty-three. No one's the same after two years, Philip.

Now: you, of course, are the man at the bus-stop."

Pulled back to the problem of the moment, Philip carefully told her the story as he knew it.

When he had finished she said slowly, "You think Irene Maxwell was keeping back something she knew all the time?"

"Not exactly. I think when I saw her the first time, she didn't know anything — or at least couldn't remember anything of consequence. But when she came here to tell me she'd just remembered that the link between the two girls was the fact they attended the same school, she'd remembered something else. On that occasion, I'm sure now, she was not telling me all she knew, or all she *thought* she knew. That's why I'm afraid she may have tried her hand at blackmail. She talked about money and wasn't at all dismayed when I told her I didn't think she'd get a share of any reward money, if and when such reward was offered, because her information would hardly lead to an arrest."

He rubbed the back of his neck in a gesture she remembered.

"Damn it, I may have pushed her toward blackmail by telling her that, but at the time I didn't believe she really knew anything. I was busy, and I didn't bother to *think*."

"You think she may have been willing to sell her information to the highest bidder, and when she found out the Law wasn't likely to bid very high, she tried another source?"

Penny made a slight grimace. "Your Irene doesn't sound a very nice character."

"No." He looked thoughtful. "Yet she wasn't as unsavoury as I'm painting her. I think she wanted the murderer caught. If she knew who he was, she'd have given him away, in time. But I think she wouldn't have seen anything wrong in making a little something on the side out of him in the meantime. She was a strange mixture of very alert and very stupid and a little greedy, but not bad. If I'm right at all."

"Why should she tell you the girls went to the same school when they didn't?" Penny mused. "Do you think she was just making it up? Perhaps as an excuse to come here and ask you about the little

97

matter of a possible reward?"

"No, I didn't think so at the time. I think perhaps — just perhaps — she believed that, and knew something else as well, something much more conclusive, and she wanted to give the police a tip — through me — while still keeping the most vital piece of information for her own purposes."

"Then," Penny said, "if she genuinely thought they attended the same school. she must have had a reason."

"Oh, she had. She'd just seen the picture of Shirley Philbrook in the old newspaper. Same uniform, she said. The only trouble with that little piece of information," he added bitterly, "is that it couldn't possibly have been the same uniform. So where does that leave us?"

"It leads me with my first assignment," Penny said briskly. "Maybe the uniforms of the two schools are similar. Tomorrow I begin chasing back-copies of newspapers. She didn't obligingly mention which paper, I suppose?" she added wistfully.

"No. Yes, hang on: she said the one with the big pages."

"Oh, thank you, Irene," Penny said

cheerfully, and then stopped in sudden dead silence. She saw Philip turn his head enquiringly. "Sorry," she said. "Just for a second it really hit me that I almost knew Irene Maxwell — really hit me that she was a human being. Stupid she may have been, and greedy, and none too scrupulous; but she didn't deserve to be thrown out of that window. If she was."

"No," Philip agreed quietly, "I don't think she deserved it, either. If she was."

"Well," Penny said, standing up, "I'll let you know if the pages of our morning daily reveal anything of note to my discerning gaze. That way we'll at least know if Irene was genuine in that respect, even if mistaken. I mightn't unearth anything tomorrow, though. I only have my lunch-hour. So don't be impatient if I don't call back for a few days. Goodnight, Philip."

And she was gone before he realized she was going.

★ ★ ★

The man casually leaned his elbow on the armrest of the driver's door while he held his afternoon paper. His hat was tipped forward at a lackadaisical angle and dark glasses would have prevented the keenest observer from noting whether or not he was reading his paper, even if anyone had been interested.

The children pouring· in chattering, eager confusion from the school-grounds were not interested. He looked like a father waiting boredly to pick up his children, relaxed and half-asleep in the warm autumn sun.

There was no one to notice that he was not half-asleep; or that his eyes followed only the girls. There was no one to notice him suddenly stiffen to attention when, as the numbers of youngsters were beginning to thin out, one girl came out alone, walking crisply and with a rather mature confidence.

A girl of thirteen, thin and of average height, mid-fair hair showing under her school hat. She had a pointed, elfin chin and lively brown eyes behind dark-rimmed glasses: not a pretty child, but one with a face that was full of personality.

The man smiled to himself. A face, he

reflected, one was not likely to forget.

Forcing himself to move casually, not to reveal a trace of the excitement and urgency that danced along his nerves, he put down his newspaper and stepped out of the car. He didn't speak to the girl or move toward her, but instead stopped a group of boys who came out a few moments behind her.

"Excuse me, boys, but can you tell me if that girl just crossing the street is Joan Barton? She's a friend of my daughter's and I was supposed to pick her up from school, but I've only met her once and can't be sure I'd know her again."

The boys paused in their own conversation to glance with disinterest at the girl. "No, that's Julie Parker," one of them said. "Joan who, did you say?"

"Barton."

"No. Sorry, mister, don't know her. Could be she's still coming, though; we're not last out. Any of you chaps know her?"

"No." They shook their heads.

"Well, thanks," the man said, and moved back to the car. "I may as well wait a bit longer."

He climbed back into the car and, the moment the boys were out of sight, turned on the ignition and drew out from the kerb, all his movements casual and disinterested. If the boys had seen him, or any passer-by had overheard his conversation, they would have seen only a mildly irritated father giving up waiting for his daughter's friend.

He drove neither hurriedly nor too slowly down the street in the direction Julie Parker had gone and drove past where she waited at a bus-stop. Fifty metres down the street there was a public telephone booth and he stopped near it and went in, dialled a number, pressed Button A and proceeded to hold a conversation for the benefit of anyone who might chance to notice him or to be within hearing. There was nothing to tell anyone that the voice at the other end of the line was a recorded one which told him the correct time at precise intervals.

The fact that he leaned easily against the wall of the booth and faced down the street was totally unremarkable. There could not have seemed to be anything more than coincidence in the fact that as a bus pulled in to the stop and the little girl with dark-rimmed glasses boarded it, along with several other school-children, the man said cheerfully, "Right. Thanks. See you," into the telephone, and hung up.

He went to his car briskly but without haste, and took out a cigarette and lit it before he drove off in the same direction as the bus. Certainly no one on the bus would have noticed or remembered the neatly-dressed man in the unremarkable white sedan which just happened to be travelling the same route as the bus, sometimes a little ahead, sometimes dropping back behind it.

Julie Parker was the only passenger to leave the bus at her stop, turning on the tree-dotted footpath to smile and wave to the driver as if they *were* old friends. Probably, the man thought idly to himself as he turned into the side street she turned into and parked his car by the kerb, they were old friends. Julie looked like the kind of kid who had friends everywhere. He thought it quite dispassionately, with no more emotion than if he were noting that the dahlias were flowering late this year.

He sat easily in his car, taking his time over extracting another cigarette from the packet and lighting it. There were City Council workmen digging a hole in the footpath on the other side of the street. The man didn't bother to wonder why they were digging it and, later, had they been questioned, the workmen would not have remembered the man in the car. He was as unremarkable to them as they were to him, and so remained, for the purposes of being remembered, virtually invisible.

Fifty metres from the corner a black dog whose appearance suggested a retriever branch in his family tree was sitting on the front lawn of a pleasant but undistinguished house. His tail had begun to sweep happily back and forth in a grass-brushing movement as soon as Julie had appeared and now he rushed at the one-and-a-third-metre fence and cleared it with obviously practised ease. Julie put down her case of books and, laughing delightedly, flung her arms around his neck and hugged him.

"You villain, Joss! Don't you teach Benny how to get over that fence. He mightn't be as smart at keeping off the street as you are. Come on. Where'd you leave Benny, anyway?"

As if in answer to her query, a tousled-haired little boy ran with a three-year-old's slightly uncertain steps to grasp the bars of the front gate and grin with wide delight at his sister's return. Julie opened the gate, hugged Ben much as she had hugged the dog, and went into the house accompanied by both.

Eldest of the family, the man in the car decided; that helped to account for her mature air. He started the car again and drove away, slowing only fractionally as he passed the house to note the number. He stopped the car again after he had turned the next corner, took a notebook from his pocket and wrote:

"Julie Parker. 24 Westport Road."

He put the notebook away and drove off, smiling. The stupid fools of police and newspaper men would call it a random crime. Random! How little they knew of the care and planning! It wasn't as if just any girl would do. Not for him. He was different — very different indeed.

It would have been very satisfactory if it could have been today, but there was no particular hurry. It would be soon. It was all a matter of waiting for the perfect opportunity, and then moving swiftly. It was simple enough if one were intelligent about it, and not too impatient.

He was a patient man.

6

TWO nights after she had been to visit him Penny phoned Philip, and her voice had an undertone of excitement.

"Irene Maxwell was genuine, I think, Philip; just mistaken in thinking back on it. Shirley Philbrook and Linda Benmore didn't attend the same school, and their school uniforms are not alike. I checked. But Miss Maxwell wasn't dreaming and she wasn't lying to create a sensation. You said she'd just been reading about Shirley Philbrook's death in an old paper when she saw the car pick Linda up?"

"Yes."

"Well, the story of Shirley's disappearance — which presumably is the one Irene was reading, since the next day's report on the discovery of her body was given much less publicity and no photographs — carried a picture of Shirley. But she wasn't in a school uniform. She was wearing the uniform of a Girl Guide. So I wondered.

"So I rang the police — one of those anonymous calls they get driven berserk by in cases like this."

She gave the sudden, quicksilver laugh he remembered so sharply. There had always been a dancing, mercurial quality about her every movement. And yet she had, too, a quality of stillness which could fall about her like a soft cloak and wrap her in a deep tranquility that gave a restfulness to anyone with her.

But the memory no more than flickered through his mind. He was too concentrated on what she had to say to give thought to pointless remembering.

She went on: "I said I had information for the homicide division and when the fellow there answered I said, 'I think I might have some information about that little girl — Linda Benmore — what got murdered.' 'Yes, madam, and what is your name, please?' 'Never you mind what my name is, young man. Just tell me this: was the child wearing a green school uniform the day she was killed?' 'No, madam, she was wearing

Girl Guide uniform. Why, madam?' And madam says sadly, 'Oh, well, it couldn't 'ave been 'er, then,' and hangs up."

Philip laughed. "You crazy twit! Why couldn't you have just rung up, said who you were, and asked nicely if both girls were Guides?"

She chuckled. "And have them tell me firmly though politely to mind my own business? I thought the gambit positively brilliant. Crazy twit indeed!"

He said slowly after a moment, "You think that was really the only thing connecting the girls? The only thing that made Irene Maxwell say that when she saw the car pick Linda up it reminded her of the Shirley Philbrook thing?"

"I just don't know, Philip. It may have been the only connection in Irene's mind. After all, it would be enough, when she saw Linda in an identical uniform, to remind her of the picture she'd been looking at a few seconds before. I think we have to accept that there probably is no sinister link between the three deaths — or even two of them."

Her voice was sober and quiet, and something in it made him nod a brief acknowledgement of her opinion. "In other words, I'm stirring mare's nests."

"No." Her tone lost none of its seriousness. "At least, not necessarily. Because it isn't really enough to explain away what you felt was a complete change in Irene's attitude; and it does produce the possibility that Linda and Shirley knew each other. I don't even know why that could be significant," she admitted. "It's all much too vague and nebulous, But — well, it does just leave a 'maybe' in my mind."

"And in mine."

"Well, then," Penny suggested cautiously, "do you suppose we could talk to the parents? I mean, if you explain who you are, and that you feel a kind of personal responsibility because the man took Linda while you were there, they mightn't mind. At the worst, all they can do is throw us out. I'll bring my car around and take you, if you can find out where the Benmores and the Philbrooks live."

"We'd have to look up the phone book, I guess. I'd not like to ask the police."

"All right. Hang on, I'll do it now."

He heard pages rustle and then: "There's a K. G. Benmore near you — Willersly Street. The Benmores first?"

He hesitated. "I don't like to intrude on them. And I must confess I don't even know what questions to ask."

"Whether the girls knew each other would do for a start."

"The police told me they didn't."

"Ah, but it's funny how much more people will say off the record. Look, boy, don't try to discourage me. My feet are cold enough as it is."

He smiled to himself at her unthinking use of the nickname she had so often used when she was teasing him or urging him to do something: Come on, boy, you can handle it; look here, boy, do you think you —

"Would you rather I pulled out of this and just left you to handle it alone, Philip?" Her present voice at the other end of the line cut in on the voice of memory. "The truth, please." There was no emotion of any kind in her voice. She was simply brisk and businesslike.

"No!" he said sharply. "I need your help. But if you feel you'd rather pull out — "

"I most certainly would rather pull out. Interviewing grief-stricken families has no appeal for me. But I don't believe I'd like living with that 'maybe' lurking in the back of my mind. I'll pick you up tomorrow night about seven-thirty." And she hung up.

★ ★ ★

She was punctual and they walked out to the street together, and only when they reached the car she laid a hand lightly on his arm and put his hand on the door-handle.

"It's an elderly white Morris 1100," she told him cheerfully.

"The same one?"

"The same. You remember that?"

He nodded. "I remember. Have you had the fuel gauge fixed?"

She laughed. "Of course you'd remember! A frantic phone-call dragged you half-way to Mt Glorious in the middle of the night when it ran out of petrol with the guage showing half, didn't it?"

"It did."

"Sorry. Yes, well, I had it fixed but I still don't trust it. Ever since, I've carried a two-gallon jerrican of petrol in the boot." Trunk

Willersly Street was only a few hundred metres away from Philip's flat. Penny stopped the car outside and told him:

"It's a medium-sized weatherboard house, well painted, white, with a red corrugated-iron roof. There's a chain-wire fence and a neat garden — roses, I can see by the street-lights, and geraniums, and the path to the front door is flat flagstones in a lawn. Will you be cross if I take your arm?"

He grinned suddenly. "It would be better than having to let you pick me out of the rose-bushes."

She locked the car and came to stand beside him. For a moment she was quite still and silent and he turned his head enquiringly toward where he knew she was standing.

"Philip," she said unexpectedly, "take off those dark glasses."

He stiffened.

"You don't need them," she said quietly.

He said with savage bitterness, "I don't wear them against the glare."

"I know why you wear them. Well, maybe there are two reasons. First, because they help people to realize that you're blind. That's a valid reason for wearing them some of the time."

Her voice was still even and quiet, refusing to be shaken by his anger. "The second and principal reason is that you're afraid of the way you look — afraid your eyes are blank, or don't track, or look grotesque in some way. You needn't be. They're as alive as ever. And they sparkle when you smile, and change your face. Don't hide that from people."

"What the hell makes you think I care how I look?" he snapped. "And how do you know what I look like without dark glasses?"

"You weren't wearing them the other night when I called at your flat. You weren't expecting visitors. You didn't look half so fearsome as you do tonight. Please take them off for now."

He hesitated, and she said simply, "Philip, do you think I'm so cruel as to lie to you about it?"

He shook his head and put the glasses in his pocket. One day, he reflected, he'd ask her how in hell she knew how much he'd wondered what his sightless eyes looked like, and how she knew the easy way to tell him.

The man who opened the door in answer to Penny's ring was a shortish, nuggety man of perhaps forty-five, with thinning dark hair. He eyed the couple on his doorstep with suspicion and a resentment he didn't try to hide.

"Yes?" he said tersely.

"Mr Benmore?" Philip spoke quickly but quietly. "My name's Philip Blair. This is Miss Cosgrove. I'm so very sorry to trouble you, and we will certainly go away at once if you wish. But I'm the man who was at the bus-stop when Linda was picked up. I — it all sounds crazy, but I have a feeling the police may be overlooking something I feel is important. Could I talk to you for a few minutes? You see, though I only talked to Linda for perhaps five minutes, I felt I knew her. I guess she was like that. I feel in a way responsible, because if I'd been able to see, the man wouldn't have dared to pick her up. I don't want him to get away, Mr Benmore."

Ken Benmore hesitated, and his tired eyes went to Penny's anxious face.

"Come in, Mr Blair," he said after a long moment. "I don't want him to get away, either. Even though it can't do Linda any good, it might save some other youngster — Come in."

He led the way across a small concrete-floored porch to a lounge-room where a small electric radiator glowed and a slight, wispy woman a few years younger than her husband knitted while she watched television. She looked up in surprise that held a strong hint of wariness, but she smiled a smile that didn't chase the tension from her face and at once switched off the television set.

Her husband explained briefly who Philip and Penny were, and the smile vanished and the stress-lines deepened. "Is there anything more to talk about?" she asked wearily.

"Mr Blair seems to think so, Joan. I think perhaps we should listen to what he has to say."

"Surely it's police business. I'm sure

116

they've asked all the questions — " She stopped herself as her voice began to rise distressedly. "I'm sorry. Yes, of course, Mr Blair, we'll do anything we can."

Philip felt a swift surge of admiration for her. He said at once, "I'm sure the police are doing an infinitely better job than I could ever do. But there's something they don't consider important, and I feel it may be. Just *may* be."

Sitting on the sofa, he told them of his meeting with Linda, and his interviews with Irene Maxwell. "Mrs Benmore," he asked gently, "why was Linda wearing Guide uniform that day?"

"It was part of a school project," Joan Benmore explained. "Each one was to take along evidence of any hobby or special interest, and anyone with a uniform — like Scouts or Guides or Army cadets — was to wear the special uniform."

Philip nodded. "I see. Do you know if Linda knew a girl named Shirley Philbrook? She was also a Guide."

"Shirley." Mrs Benmore considered. "No, I don't think so. Do you remember, Ken?"

117

"No. Can't say I ever remember Linda speaking of her. I can't say for sure, of course, that she never did, but I'd say definitely they weren't close friends or anything like that. I seem to remember the police asked us about that girl, too. Why the interest in her?"

"Because Irene Maxwell insisted that the only reason she noticed Linda getting into the car that morning was because it reminded her of the newspaper report on Shirley Philbrook's disappearance. Shirley was found drowned, apparently by accident. But there doesn't seem to be any reason for Irene to have linked them, except that they were both Guides and both were reported to have got into a white or cream Holden or Falcon. It doesn't seem to me enough to link them as strongly as apparently they were linked in her mind — particularly as any idea of Shirley Philbrook going off in a car was later discounted entirely. I think Irene may have known something else she wasn't prepared to talk about to me or to the police. But although she wouldn't tell what she knew, for reasons of her own, she wanted to arouse someone's suspicion so that the idea of a link would be followed up."

Ken Benmore said slowly, "And now she's dead. That's what's bothering you?"

"That's what's bothering me. But it may be no more than a grim coincidence. I confess I can't for the life of me think what connection there could be between the deaths of the two girls."

Joan Benmore said flatly, "Maybe it's just a maniac who kills Girl Guides."

"Even that's possible, I suppose. But if Irene *did* know something special, I think there must have been some connection between the two girls."

"Did this other little girl — Shirley — live near here?"

"No. Right over Indooroopilly way."

"Then I'm sure Linda wouldn't have known her."

"The two girls mightn't have belonged to the same group, or troop, or whatever Guides are called," Penny put in. "But would there be occasions when Guides from one group would meet with others from other centres?"

"Oh, yes, certainly," Mrs Benmore said.

119

Philip sat up straight suddenly. "Would there have been any such occasion, say, a month to six weeks ago?"

The Benmores looked at each other questioningly. "There was something a few weeks ago, I think," Ken said uncertainly, as if time had been taken out of the context of life and he was unsure of its meaning.

"I'll get Linda's diary," his wife said. "I can't remember, but Linda kept a diary of her Guide activities."

It was a small pocket diary she handed to Penny. "You look," she said simply, and Penny knew the unspoken explanation: "I can't look at Linda's handwriting. Not yet."

She flicked back through the pages. "Here's the entry. 'Saturday, 16th. Rally for visiting African Guides, morning. Afternoon: Take visitors on individual city tours.'" She turned more pages and then glanced at Philip. "That's the only likely entry. The sixteenth. That would be four weeks ago."

"That's right," Mrs Benmore nodded. "I do remember. Yes, of course. Linda was away the whole day. The morning

120

rally was quite a big thing, so there'd be Guides from lots of different centres. I think the afternoon part was quite informal, with the local girls entertaining their visitors as they saw fit. Then there was a sort of concert in the evening."

She looked down at her hands in her lap, her fingers twining tightly together. "We didn't go to the concert. Linda was disappointed, because she was singing. We'd never heard her sing in public. She sang nicely — folk music, that sort of thing. I had flu, and Ken didn't want to go out and leave me. We never heard her sing."

The utter lifelessness of her voice was more frightening than hysteria. Ken Benmore went and sat on the arm of her chair, his arm about her shoulders. He looked at Penny, and she nodded and stood up. Philip at once stood with her and she took his arm.

"Thank you very much," he said. "You've been very helpful. I'm sorry to have intruded."

"That's all right," Ken Benmore said quickly. "We want to do whatever we can."

"That's what the police always say," his wife said mechanically without raising her head. "We've been very helpful. But it's only words, isn't it? It doesn't do anything."

"I think it will be words that track the man down, Mrs Benmore," Philip said. "Words. When all the words that tell all that people know are put together, the answer will be there, if we can only see it. If people tell everything they know."

At the door, Ken Benmore asked: "What did you mean by that last remark, Mr Blair? Do you think someone knows something they won't tell?"

"I think Irene Maxwell knew something. But if she did, she deliberately witheld it. Other people may be keeping something back quite accidentally — simply because they don't know that it matters."

"If you want to know more about the Guide rally, get in touch with Mrs Simpson. She was leader of Linda's group. She'd know all the details."

He told them the address and they thanked him and left.

In the car Penny sat for a while without making a move to start it.

"I was looking at the house," she explained. "It looks just an ordinary house. No one would guess the people in there are living in hell."

He nodded. After a minute he said: "What made you think of the possibility Linda had met with other Guides? I know: common sense. But it was darned smart."

She smiled crookedly. "Why? It doesn't help much. Suppose Linda and Shirley did meet that day? So what? Where's the significance — if any?"

"If any. That's the wall we keep bumping into. But there might be a door in that wall, and we'd better keep looking for it. The rally was on the sixteenth. And Shirley Philbrook was drowned on the eighteenth. Two girls who might very easily have met on the sixteenth. And both are dead. And so is a rather stupid waitress who was still smart enough to think she knew something."

He frowned his concentration. "Penny, is it just coincidence?"

For a moment she didn't answer. When she did, her voice was serious. "The odds that it is are long, Philip."

"Too long?"

"I don't know."

"You think I'm barking up a tree that isn't even planted yet, don't you?"

She sighed. "Philip, I'm stuck, like the police, with one thought: how on earth can there be a connection? Why shouldn't the girls' deaths be exactly what they appeared to be — an accidental drowning and a sex-killing? What does it *matter* if the girls knew each other?"

"Why shouldn't the deaths be what they appear? Because Irene Maxwell planted the idea in my head that they were not. A stupid, self-important woman with a riotous imagination." He gritted his teeth. "Or with a cunning idea. Which? Damn it, *which*?"

He sighed. "If Shirley's death was accidental, or if Linda's was the work of a sex-maniac, then there is no connection and certainly the girls needn't have known each other. And if Irene Maxwell had still been alive I'd have been as willing as the police to dismiss her suggestions, and accept both deaths for what they appear."

Penny shook her head. "But *why*,

Philip? Why should anyone want to harm those two children — unless it were a madman?"

Philip hunched his shoulders and scowled again in thought. "Suppose — oh, damn, it's all so hypothetical. But, well, if both girls were murdered they must have been killed by the same person, and it can be for one of only two reasons. First, because they knew something. Probably something they didn't understand, but which made their knowledge dangerous to somebody."

Penny didn't speak, and he went on bitterly: "Oh, sure, as a movie plot it's been done before. Stop me if it's getting boring."

"Philip," she said quietly, "I'm on your team, remember? You don't have to fight me."

He turned his head toward her. "Sorry. The thing's so crazy I get angry with myself for even thinking about it. But what I'm trying to say is that if the two girls were killed by the same person, it was no run-of-the-mill sex-killer — if any are run-of-the-mill. So — well, suppose they see somebody they know coming out of

Number Three Billington Street carrying a longish, narrow object wrapped in a towel. It doesn't mean anything to them because they don't know that someone inside has just been shot. But they've seen the murderer; they're dangerous to him; they have to go."

"*Was* there a shooting in Billington Street?"

"Of course not, you prize ass. I don't even know if there is a Billington Street. All I'm trying to say is that something like that could have happened. Something like that could be the reason the two girls died. But if they did see or hear something that was deadly dangerous to somebody — so dangerous he was prepared to kill to ensure silence — it was something they didn't understand. I mean, they didn't rush home shouting: 'Hey, Mum, we just saw Mr Brown chuck a body in the river!'"

"Actually, you know," Penny said thoughtfully, "they just might have done something like that, and their parents dismissed the thing as too ridiculous. Kids aren't always taken as seriously as they should be. Perhaps we should ask the Benmores whether Linda mentioned anything unusual happening."

She added quickly, "Not tonight. They've had enough. But some other time. They wouldn't really mind. They want to help. Anyway, we're going to see the Philbrooks too, aren't we? We can ask them."

"We can ask her. There is no Mr P., apparently."

"Dead?"

"Left home."

"And Mrs Philbrook's only child is dead? Life's being pretty cruel to her, isn't it? And now a couple of amateur sleuths turn up on her doorstep and announce that they think maybe her daughter was murdered. If she doesn't throw us out of the house it'll be a miracle. When do we go to see her? Make it tomorrow night, will you? Before my nerve gives out entirely."

"Penny — "

"Don't offer to let me off the hook, boy, because if you do I'll bolt like the devil was after me. And I don't really want to prove to myself what a rotten coward I am."

He said gently, "It's not cowardly to want to avoid hurting people."

There was a silence and then Penny, sounding as if she had come back against her will from somewhere a long way off, said:

"You said that if Irene Maxwell was right and both girls were killed, and by the same man, it had to be for one of only two reasons. One, they knew something which made them too dangerous to be left alive. What is the second reason?"

"It occurred to me," he said grimly, "that it could be something like Mrs Benmore's suggestion: he's a maniac who kills only Girl Guides."

She sat for a little while, and then started the car. "Then we'd better start finding out what crimes occurred on the sixteenth of last month, and consider whether any of them might have been witnessed by the girls; and whether any were serious enough to make the criminal turn killer."

"The most likely reason he'd kill would be that he was a killer already," Philip mused. "And of course, it mightn't have been the crime itself they saw. They might have seen the disposal of evidence, or something like that."

"Mr Brown chucking a body in the river."

"Exactly. Or a gun, or an axe, or whatever. So we have to look at crimes that were committed not only that day, but for maybe a week before."

"Oh, great. And how do we go about that? Are you friendly with the inspector?"

"Not very, I'm afraid. I've worn out my welcome. I could try, but it looks as though it's back to the old newspapers for you."

"Thank you. I trust my salary will be suitably adjusted?"

He grinned suddenly. "You know, I'd forgotten what a miserable skin-flint you were."

"Ha," she said derisively. "With a charming line like that you must really get along."

They drove the rest of the way back to his flat in silence, but it was an easy, companionable silence. They both knew they were being flippant in defence against the monstrous thought that would swamp their minds if they allowed it. The thought of a madman killing at random, or even according to a pattern that made sense to him alone, was frightening.

But it was nothing when compared with the thought of a man who was not mad, but would coolly kill two children who somehow got in his way.

7

NEXT afternoon as Philip arrived home he was waylaid by Marcia Feldman.

After solicitous questions about his work she said, "Philip, darling, I'm simply *bursting* with curiosity. That very soap-and-water-wholesome young lady who's been here a few times — *who* ever is she?"

"By name Penelope Cosgrove, by profession a pharmaceutical chemist, by request an assistant unpaid private investigator," Philip said cheerfully.

"Is *that* it? Darling!" Marcia cried triumphantly. "You mean you're doing your own investigations in that awful murder? But how exciting!"

"It isn't, as a matter of fact," Philip said soberly. "It's unhappy and depressing and probably totally futile."

"Do you think you have a clue to the killer's identity?" Marcia asked breathlessly.

"Unfortunately, not the slightest. Excuse me, won't you — I'm awfully sorry, but I'm in a hurry."

Marcia remained standing where she was for a minute, a distant look on her face. She didn't hear her husband's approach until he spoke.

"What'd your pet school-master have to say to send you into a trance?"

For once the sarcasm didn't register. "He and that girl who's been here a couple of times are investigating the murder of that little girl. I wonder why he's doing it?"

"Well, he isn't likely to get far, is he? A blind man playing detective?"

"He may be blind, but he's a clever man," Marcia retorted.

"Oh, it's plain to everyone *you* think he's superman — always running after him. It's sickening, it's so obvious. I'll bet you sleep with him when I'm not here!"

She turned her head slowly to look at him in contempt.

"My dear, I'll sleep with him when you *are* here if I choose."

"Everyone can see you're crazy about

him. That green-eyed girl had better watch out. It wouldn't surprise me if *you* pushed his sexy little waitress out of that window." The cunning look of the half-drunk came over his face. "Where *were* you that night, anyway?"

Anger flared in her eyes. "I'd be more interested to know where *you* were the day Linda Benmore disappeared. Maybe Philip Blair should know it wouldn't be the first time you'd been accused of playing around with young girls."

"It was that child's word against mine!" he snapped. "She was a lying, precocious brat and I never tried to lay a hand on her."

Marcia looked at him for a long, cold minute. "Of course," she said eventually — and managed to make the words damning.

She turned and went into their flat and left him standing uncertainly for a while before he followed her.

* * *

Later in the evening when Philip answered the doorbell, instead of the wispy fragrance of Penny's perfume, he was greeted by a rather heavy smell of rum.

"Evening, Philip," his neighbour's slightly blurred voice said.

"Oh, Max. Are you coming in?"

"Thank you — very kind of you, but I don't want to keep you." He walked in nevertheless and sat in Philip's favourite chair. Forty, above average in height, he had probably been good-looking when Marcia had married him. But the looks now were weak and the figure was running to alcohol fat.

"Fact is, old man, I wondered — well, you're working with the police on the murder of that little girl, aren't you?"

Philip smiled. "Nothing so grand, Max. The police don't like me very much. It's just that I have a theory of my own I want to follow up."

Max shook his head sadly. "The police don't like me, either."

Philip waited.

"They've been asking me questions," Max blurted out.

"What sort of questions?"

"Like where I was that morning. I was out in my car trying to sell insurance like

I always am, but I can't prove it. What did Marcia tell you about me?"

Philip shook his head. "Nothing special that I can recall."

"She's here a lot, isn't she?"

"Your wife's quite kind to me," Philip said carefully.

"I'll bet."

Philip had left the door open and Max said now, his manner ingratiating again, "You've got a visitor, I see. Must be off." He went toward the door and then turned. "Why are they asking me questions?"

Philip said smilingly, "Max, it's routine. They're questioning every man in the streets between here and the bus-stop who could know I was blind. That's all."

"Oh. Oh, is that it!" He sounded relieved, then added anxiously, "They keep records, though, don't they?" He nodded to Penny. "Evening, miss," and went.

"Who's that rather unpleasant little man?" Penny asked.

"Max Walsh. Insurance salesman, married to Marcia Feldman who is a

135

presently-out-of-work actress. They live next door."

"Oh, the tall lady with headscarves and earrings who so carefully watches me come and go. What on earth was he so upset about?"

Philip rubbed the back of his neck. "I don't know. Just sozzled and wanting to wail, I think. The police — for the reasons I gave him — have been asking him where he was when Linda was killed. It seems to have gravely insulted him."

"Doesn't seem the type to make much of a salesman."

"No. Well, hardly as predatory as his wife."

Penny laughed. "Does she hunt you?"

"With the determination of a Bengal tigress."

"Really? I'll bet you struggle madly."

He grinned and Penny came in and closed the door and asked, "Did you try the police for that list of crimes?"

"I did, feeling I was taking my life in my hands."

"Were you?"

"More or less. Inspector Batlow is a very patient man, but he very naturally wishes people would allow police to do police work — a sentiment I heartily echo, except that just this once I think they may be mistaken. Anyway, I called Des again this evening, and he promised to check up for me. How did you make out with the newspapers?"

"I couldn't find anything significant. I only had time to cover the papers of the seventeenth and back to the fifteenth. There was a stabbing in South Brisbane — hotel brawl at eleven at night, hardly the sort of thing two Guides would get mixed up with. Plenty of witnesses, anyway. And a non-fatal shooting in Spring Hill — fellow loosed a twenty-two at his wife's boyfriend; all very quickly solved. Apart from those, only petty stuff — breaking and entering, and only on a fairly small scale."

He frowned. "Well, keep going back for a few days, would you? It must be something big enough to make the newspapers, or it wouldn't be enough to warrant murder."

She said gravely, "We mightn't think it was enough to warrant murder. But how do we know how the murderer thinks? If he killed two children, he's not exactly soft-hearted. There are plenty of cases on record where people have killed for a paltry few dollars."

"It's not just a matter of callousness, though. There's the question of risk. No matter how unfeeling he might be, he wouldn't want to take unnecessary chances. One murder was a big enough risk. Two — if there were two — enormously increased the risk."

"And if there were three?"

"The stakes would have to be very high indeed to warrant it."

"Well, I'll keep hunting, and Des may come up with something."

He nodded. "Perhaps. Though I can't help feeling Des doesn't take me very seriously. But he did give me Mrs Philbrook's address."

★ ★ ★

Adelaide Philbrook's residence, Penny explained to him as they drew up in front of it, was different from the Benmore's. To begin with it was in a more fashionable area, and secondly it had cost a good deal more to build — brick and tiles and every indication of a gardener.

"I understand she has a private income," Philip said.

"Well, she's not living on Social Security."

She was silent for a moment and Philip said, "What are you thinking?"

She took a long breath. "That somehow I can't see Adelaide Philbrook's only child playing hookey from school to go fishing in the river with a line wrapped around a Coke bottle. I just felt a queer kind of prickling in the back of my neck. I think, Philip, for the first time I believe your waitress friend may have been on to something."

When Penny rang the doorbell Philip murmured, "Who opens the door to callers — the maid or the mistress of the house?"

"I'll give you two to one the maid," Penny breathed back.

But the woman who opened the door was clearly not the maid. Philip didn't need to be able to see the tall, blond woman with an air of elegance that was due only in minor part to the simple but expensive clothes she wore with the unawareness of someone who always dressed that way. The breath of French perfume told him even before the cool and cultured voice asked distantly:

"Yes?"

"Good evening, Mrs Philbrook," he said at once. "I'm Philip Blair. This is Miss Cosgrove. You'll remember I telephoned you this afternoon to ask for an appointment."

"Of course," Mrs Philbrook acknowledged. "Come in, please."

Penny took Philip's arm as Mrs Philbrook led them into a spacious livingroom furnished with taste and at considerable expense.

She sat in a high-backed easy-chair, cool blue eyes watching Penny very unobtrusively guide Philip to the lounge. There was a breath of cold amusement in Adelaide Philbrook's voice:

"I understood you were a private detective, Mr Blair."

"I said I was engaged on some private investigations. I'm not a private detective."

"So I gather, since a blind man would hardly be fitted for the work. Oh, you handle your handicap very well, but it's not one it's possible to conceal. Now then, Mr Blair let us be frank. I suspect you deliberately allowed me to assume you were a private detective."

"I suppose I did. I didn't deliberately mislead you, Mrs Philbrook, but I admit I was quite willing to let you reach a wrong conclusion — though only because being mistaken for a private detective gave me some chance of an interview. Being a rank amateur made me just another nut to have the door slammed in his face. And I felt it was very important that you should allow us to talk to you."

She studied him with cool deliberation for some seconds, and then nodded. "Very well, since you're here, I'm prepared to hear what you have to say. You said it was a matter which may have involved my daughter."

Philip began, "I'm truly sorry to bring the thing all back to — "

"Just say what you have to say, Mr Blair."

He nodded. "Have you ever heard Shirley mention another Guide named Linda Benmore?"

It was impossible to tell by the few seconds silence whether Adelaide Philbrook was remembering what had happened to Linda Benmore, or whether she was simply trying to recall whether she had ever heard the name.

"I don't remember her having done so. I can't say she didn't. Certainly they weren't close friends."

"I see. Would you remember if Shirley attended a rally for visiting Guides from some African countries on the sixteenth of last month?"

"She did." With a seemingly casual movement Mrs Philbrook brought her hands together in her lap to intertwine the fingers.

Philip felt Penny move slightly on the sofa beside him and thought the movement was one of excitement: Shirley and Linda had been together two days before Shirley died. Two weeks before Linda did.

But a moment later he realized Penny had turned in surprise, for a man's voice spoke with an unexpectedness that made Philip start slightly, just as his sudden appearance in the doorway that opened from the lounge-room into a hallway had made Penny jump.

"Who are these people, Addy? Police?"

He was a big man of about thirty-five, straight fair hair cut short, light blue eyes prominent in a slightly puffy face with a tell-tale slackness about it which wiped out Penny's first instinctive thought that this must be Adelaide Philbrook's lover.

Mrs Philbrook looked fleetingly annoyed, but at once smiled. "No, William, of course not. This is Miss Cosgrove, and Mr Blair. My brother, William Ford. I thought you were watching television, William. I wish you wouldn't wear those sneakers — I never hear you walking and you positively make me jump."

She said it indulgently and William grinned and looked pleased.

It was quite right, Penny thought: for a big man he walked with remarkable silence.

"I was watching TV, but I heard voices and I could tell someone was asking questions. About Shirley. So I thought it must be police."

He leaned against the doorpost in a way that was curiously insolent, though Penny couldn't, to save her life, have explained why it seemed that way. He looked at her with the open interest of a child, and from her to Philip.

The thought struck her so suddenly that she asked the question almost before she knew she was going to:

"Why don't you like the police, Mr Ford?"

He shifted his feet as if getting into a better defensive stance and said sullenly, "I never said I didn't."

But even more revealing was the way Adelaide Philbrook's face froze into instant blankness.

William looked at her and said, "Why are they asking questions about Shirley?"

"As a matter of fact, William," she said smoothly, "I was about to ask Mr Blair that, just as you came in."

Philip said slowly into the small silence, "Because someone told me that there was some connection between your daughter and Linda Benmore. The police weren't

144

interested. I was."

Adelaide Philbrook looked faintly puzzled, but her brother said sharply, "What's Shirley got to do with her?"

"It may not be important at all. I hope it isn't."

Mrs Philbrook said, "Mr Blair, will you kindly stop talking in riddles? Why should my daughter have any connection, as you put it, with this other girl? And why should the police be interested? And beyond all, what precisely is *your* interest?"

"To answer the last question first, Mrs Philbrook, I was the only other person at a bus-stop when Linda Benmore, who was the same age as your daughter, was given a lift in a car. Later that day she was found murdered. Since I am blind, I couldn't identify the man who abducted her — neither the man nor the car. If you think about that, and how I might feel, you may come up with at least some kind of answer."

Adelaide Philbrook was staring at him, a struggling apprehension tightening her face. "Go on," was all she said.

"A waitress in a milk-bar near the

bus-stop saw the car but said she took no notice and could offer no sort of description. Later, she strongly insinuated to me that she believed Linda's and your daughter's deaths had a connection, I don't know what the connection was, if any. That's what I want to find out."

"That," Adelaide Philbrook said in icy fury, "is the lowest of cheap sensationalism. My daughter died in a tragic accident. Surely that was bad enough. What you are suggesting is monstrous. I should hope the police would not be interested in your disgusting inferences. I must ask you please to go."

Philip and Penny at once stood up. Philip said firmly, "Of course we'll go. But you see, Mrs Philbrook, Shirley and Linda attended the same Guide rally. So there was at least some connection."

"Then why don't you ask your waitress informant what the connection was?" She moved ahead of them to the door.

"Because," he said quietly, "she died, in another tragic accident. She fell from a high window."

Adelaide Philbrook had her hand

stretched out to the knob of the front door. As if the knob had been electrified she snatched her hand away, stood for several seconds absolutely still, and then turned her head to look at Penny. Penny nodded.

In a different voice that had lost its assurance and was strangely old, Adelaide Philbrook said:

"Ask your questions, Mr Blair. I'll answer. But if you have done this for nothing, never let me see you again."

Philip gave a little nod of acknowledgement. "I understand you felt at the time that it was out of character for Shirley to play truant from school?"

"Yes. There must have been some quite extraordinary reason for her to do it. I never found out what it was — possibly she was worried about an exam, or had had a quarrel with one of her school friends. I never found out. If she hadn't wished to go to school that day for any reason I do not understand why she didn't discuss it with me. We had a good relationship."

She spoke rapidly, as if anxious to get it over.

"Was Shirley keen on fishing?"

"No."

"Not at all?"

"Not at all. She'd had plenty of chances to go fishing — on holidays and so on. I only once recall her going fishing with her grandfather. She was most unenthusiastic about the experience."

"Yet she played hookey and went fishing."

"Yes." Adelaide Philbrook's chin lifted slightly in defiance.

"You're quite sure of that?"

"Of course I'm sure. I have to accept the obvious evidence for which there is no other explanation."

Philip said slowly, "The place where Shirley was found is quite a distance from here. How do you suppose she got there?"

"I presume she walked. After all, it was only a matter of a mile or so."

"When Shirley was reported missing and it was made public, I understand there were many reports from people who said they had seen her."

Adelaide Philbrook was watching him coldly. She made no move to suggest they might go back to the loungeroom and sit down.

"I believe such reports are all too common in the case of missing persons," she said. "All of them proved false."

Philip raised an eyebrow. "Then no one reported seeing her walking toward the area where she was found?"

"Evidently not. Why should anyone notice? She'd be just walking along the street, simply another schoolgirl: who would notice?"

"Oh, I see the point, Mrs Philbrook. It just seems rather strange that not one of the many people who must have seen her — walking in the opposite direction from the school she attended — recalled it. On the other hand, there were reports that she had been seen getting into cars or on to motor-cycles."

"All those reports obviously were false."

"Can you be certain?" he asked gently.

Her eyes blazed anger but her voice was steady. "I can be certain. Not one report held the least suggestion that force was used to get Shirley to enter a car or do any of the other things people thought they'd seen. And she would never have gone with a stranger of her own accord. That I most certainly do know."

"I see." He frowned. "Mrs Philbrook, when Shirley came home from the rally — or whatever name it goes by — on the sixteenth, did she talk about it?"

"Yes, naturally."

"Could you remember anything of what she said? What the girls did?"

"I'm afraid I really wouldn't have taken a great deal of notice. I don't know very much about Guide activities."

She seemed about to leave her answer at that, but Penny saw her look at Philip and study his face with its intense, concentrated look.

"The morning," Adelaide Philbrook added, "was spent fairly routinely, I believe, in displaying Guide activities for the benefit of the visiting African Guides. There was a picnic-type lunch, I think, and some local girls were asked to spend the afternoon showing Brisbane to their guests in their own way. That part was designed to display initiative or something. The day wound up with a barbecue tea about five-thirty and a concert afterwards. I brought Shirley home about ten-thirty."

"The afternoon." Philip's tone was almost urgent. "Do you remember what Shirley did?"

"She was one of those who took the visitors sight-seeing. I don't know any details."

"Please, Mrs Philbrook. Try to remember. Perhaps Shirley would have talked about it — that night, for instance, as you were coming home in the car."

She was still watching him closely, as if trying to guess what he was thinking. Abruptly she turned her head away as if to hide the emotion that might show in her face — forgetful for the moment that she need not hide it from a blind man.

Penny touched Philip's arm restrainingly, and he waited in silence.

"Yes," Adelaide Philbrook said presently, carefully straightening a fold in a curtain. "Yes, she did talk rather a lot on the way home. I didn't take much notice. I was busy with the traffic."

Her hands suddenly clenched the curtain fabric and she said harshly, "My daughter talked to me. She had less than forty-eight hours to live and she talked to me and I didn't even listen because I thought she would be there somewhere to talk to me for forty years. Why do you make me remember?"

Philip said very gently after a moment, "Did she mention anything unusual that happened that day?"

Mrs Philbrook let go of the curtain and turned to look at him, in full control of herself again.

"Unusual? In what way unusual?"

"She didn't mention anything that upset her, or puzzled her?"

"I don't think so."

"She took part in showing the African girls around the city. Can you remember anything she said about that — anywhere they went? It may be important."

She shook her head. "I can't recall anything in particular. I do remember," she added a little reluctantly, "that Shirley said they'd gone to see my step-father. Shirley always called him Grandpa, though he was no actual relative."

Philip looked puzzled. "Why did Shirley take the visiting Guides to see him? Is he a public figure?"

"No. My step-father is a gem merchant. If he happened to be in the right mood he would let Shirley look at some of his stock of precious stones. To her, a visit to his office was the equivalent of a trip to Aladdin's cave."

Penny felt Philip stiffen beside her, but he only said, "I suppose so. I wonder if your step-father might recall whether Shirley had spoken of anything unusual, that day? Would you mind giving us his address?"

Adelaide Philbrook obliged and Penny jotted the address down. Then they thanked her and said goodnight.

As they left, Penny glanced back into the loungeroom to say goodnight to William Ford, but he had gone. She hadn't noticed at what point he had slipped out of the room.

8

"A GEM-MERCHANT," Philip said when they were back in the car. "Now suppose the girls witnessed a theft there?"

"But that sort of theft would have made the newspapers," Penny reminded him.

He sighed. "I suppose so. Unless for some reason it was hushed up. If it was, Des will know. But damn it, Penny those two girls *were* together that day. Oh, sure, so were several hundred others, no doubt. But it lifts the possibility of a real link."

"Are you going to tell the police?"

He shook his head. "What do I have to tell? That Linda and Shirley and a few hundred other girls were more or less together a couple of days before Shirley drowned? What does it mean? Why on earth should it mean anything?"

"You could contact that Guide leader Mr Benmore spoke of — find out whether anyone would know who went with whom on the show-your-city tour bit."

"I'll do that. What did you make of Mrs Philbrook?"

"That we'd better not go back without a darned good reason. Her daughter was accidentally drowned. That's enough for her to have to live with. That's the way she wants it to stay."

"I can't blame her. But I'd like to talk to the step-father. Will you be in it?"

"Try shaking me off." She put the key in the ignition and then paused. "I don't much like William."

"William? Oh, the brother. A shade simple, isn't he?"

"Yes. But not at all bad. Rather like a picture that's not quite in focus."

"Adelaide Philbrook has her share of troubles. Do you suppose he lives there?"

"Hard to say. I don't think he's so bad he'd need someone to care for him. She seems very protective toward him, and fond of him."

"Mmm. I'd like to talk to the gem-merchant at his place of business. I finish at the school at three — any chance you could leave work a bit early tomorrow afternoon?"

She started the car. "You have but to speak, and I obey."

He grinned. "Really? I never noticed the signs before." He was swiftly serious again. "You're genuinely interested now, Pen, aren't you? Why?"

"I think there are too many coincidences to be coincidence," she said slowly. "And, as I said earlier tonight — and my feeling was heightened after meeting the mother — I just can't see Adelaide Philbrook's daughter going fishing with a line around an empty Coke bottle. And, though she refuses to look at the fact, neither can Adelaide Philbrook."

On the drive back to the flat, she described Adelaide Philbrook, her house and her brother. Outside the flats, Penny told him:

"Two paces right and three forward and that's the bottom step. I'll pick you up outside the school at half-past three tomorrow."

"Thanks."

He walked forward until his cane touched the lowest of the three concrete steps which led from the footpath up to the level of the lawn in front of the building. Then he paused. There was a street-lamp just to his right, he knew — the memory so strong suddenly he could almost feel the bluish light that the lamp poured down spilling over him and along the footpath as he stood there in the darkness.

Abruptly he turned his head toward the car. "Come in for a cup of coffee?"

"No, thanks, Philip, I shan't be a nuisance. We agreed when I signed on for this job: strictly business."

"Did I sound as if being polite was an effort?"

He knew she smiled. "Yes, you did, rather. See you tomorrow. Goodnight."

He went up the steps and along the path to the front door with long, unhesitating strides. He knew she didn't start the car until he was at the door, and he felt a surge of anger. Why did she think she had to stay and watch him as if he were helpless? Did she regard him with the same protective indulgence Adelaide Philbrook showed for her slightly retarded brother?

He closed the front door with a near-slam just as the telephone rang.

In response to his curt: "Yes?" Des Maddock's voice said cheerfully:

"Sorry, old man. What did I interrupt?"

"What? Oh." Philip grinned ruefully. "I must be sounding especially bad-tempered all over the place tonight. That's all you interrupted — a fit of bad temper."

"Oh — oh."

"Meaning you're not about to tell me anything that will brighten my day?"

"Meaning just that. There's no hush-hush about crimes on or around the date you gave me. There just weren't any major ones, or not that we know of."

★ ★ ★

"And there," Philip told Penny next afternoon, "you have it. Blank wall."

"Did you phone Mrs Simpson, the Guide leader Mr Benmore spoke of?"

"I did. A bright, rather chatty lady, quite unsuspicious of my motives. But as for finding out who went where and with whom — well. About three hundred

158

girls attended the daytime thing. In the afternoon some girls were chosen to take their guests — twenty-five girls from several African nations — on tours of the city sights. If you wanted to take a visitor somewhere you had to submit a written itinerary for approval, and parents' permission also in writing. But — 'I'm sorry, Mr Blair, but Mrs Thomas was in charge of that activity, and she and her husband are overseas on a motoring tour of Europe.' So we'd better start hoping for something from Mrs Philbrook's stepfather."

Penny didn't speak for a while, and Philip said enquiringly, "Pen?"

"I was just thinking," she said quietly. "We keep hoping for clues, for leads. It's rather horrible; because if we find them, it means both children were murdered. We should be hoping we *don't* find any leads."

He said evenly, "All I want is to know they've got the man who killed Linda." He paused and then added, "I don't even know how much I want it on Linda's account and how much on mine."

He gave a laugh. "Such nobility!"

The tone was mocking, but Penny knew the frustration behind it. The thing had become symbolic. His anger against Linda's killer was his anger against his blindness: while the one defeated him, so did the other.

Penny wondered what the killer would have felt if he had known the deep-biting rage he had touched off; what his reaction would have been if he had known that a blind man was doggedly trying to follow him in the dark. She rather thought that, had he known, the murderer would have felt no more than amusement.

Just as I, she thought suddenly, feel no more than pity.

Pity. She manoeuvred the car in the inner-city traffic and thought about it. Was that all she felt — pity for Philip in his desperate need to prove himself to himself, to fight above his handicap? Pity because she felt him unequal to the task?

No. Not only pity. Respect for his determination, plus the respect she had always had for the mind, for the man. But there was something almost akin to the murderer's contempt in her conviction that, however right Philip's suspicions might be, there was an almost total futility in his efforts to prove anything.

I wonder, she thought to herself suddenly, whether I would have the same feeling of futility if Philip were not blind? I'm convinced, not that he's wrong, but that he'll fail. I dread that moment when he has to face it, because he'll hate himself for having failed, hate the world for foiling him, and hate me because I saw him fail.

He broke into her thoughts. "Traffic especially bad?"

"Just normally especially bad. Why?"

"Every other time we've been out in the car you've done a running commentary."

"Sorry. Does it annoy you?"

"No. It lets me see what's happening. I miss it." He smiled, and suddenly, violently, she wanted to cry, and she wasn't even very sure why.

She said lightly, "I'm nervous. I've never interviewed a gem-merchant before. He'll probably think we're casing the joint and call the police. Blast! No, hang on — thought we'd missed his street, but here we are. Uh-huh. Joseph Rubenstein, Precious Stones. Tell you one thing: from the outside appearance, Aladdin's cave it's not. It's a shabby, grimy industrial-type street and Mr Rubenstein has space — not much, I'd say — on the ground floor of a singularly unprepossessing building."

"Maybe the bottom's dropped out of the diamond market."

"Don't think step-father could ever have afforded diamonds. A nice bit of amethyst and the occasional zircon would be the limit, I should think."

She stopped the car and Philip said, "No parking problems?"

"No. The world, I suspect, doesn't beat a path to Mr Rubenstein's door."

She took Philip's arm and they went through a glass door marked 'Push' in paint that needed re-doing, and found themselves in a small outer office, where a well-groomed middle-aged brunette looked up from a desk that had seen better days and said, "Good afternoon. May I help?"

Penny told Philip afterwards: "The

moment she spoke I knew my deprecatory remarks about Grandpa's establishment were way off line. Any office where she works pays about three times award wages."

Philip said, "May we see Mr Rubenstein?"

"Have you an appointment?" It was said in perfect courtesy, but still managed to convey that unless you were on bona fide business you didn't get past Mr Rubenstein's secretary any more readily than you got past a ten-foot brick wall.

"No," Philip admitted. "It's a personal matter concerning his granddaughter Shirley."

Alert grey eyes behind black-rimmed glasses studied him briefly. "May I have your names?"

Philip told her, and added, "They won't mean anything to him."

She tripped an intercom switch and relayed the message, not taking her eyes off Philip and Penny.

A heavy voice that spoke in a slight accent holding the hint of a lisp came after a long pause. "Have I any appointments soon?"

"I don't think so, Mr Rubenstein."

"Very well. Ask them to come in, Mrs Frame."

Penny noted that in answering the appointments question Mrs Frame had made no move to check any appointment book or memo pad. So, she thought, Mrs Frame and her employer used it as a code: if the secretary thought you were genuine — or harmless — you got in; if she didn't, you didn't.

And, Penny felt sure, the intercom was left on so that Mrs Frame knew every word that was spoken in the inner office into which she smilingly ushered Penny and Philip.

Mr Rubenstein's office was as unimpressive as the outer one. The tall, slight man behind the desk stood up and gestured to the well-worn chairs in front of it. The desk was as untidy as his clothes and his iron-grey hair. A drooping moustache seemed to accent hollow cheeks and sunken blue eyes and, though Penny judged him to be in his late sixties, he moved like a much older man, and she guessed Jacob Rubenstein was plagued by ill-health.

But the eyes were shrewd as he looked

from one to the other.

"What have you to say of my granddaughter?" he asked bluntly, almost before they were seated.

Philip said, "We — or rather, I — will sound like some kind of nut, possibly. I can only ask you to listen to me a moment."

He swiftly outlined his meeting with Linda Benmore, and with Irene Maxwell. Joseph Rubenstein didn't move or speak and it was impossible to tell whether he was interested or about to order them off his premises.

"So," he said curtly. "This woman said there was a connection between my granddaughter's death and this Linda someone's. Well? Why should it be so, and why do you come to me?"

"We think the girls may have met. They were both Guides and there was a rally two days before Shirley was drowned. We — "

"Go to her mother to ask of her friends." He shuffled some papers on his desk impatiently. "I am a busy man and I do not know."

"We went to see Mrs Philbrook,"

Philip told him. "We know both girls attended that rally. Mrs Philbrook told us Shirley and some other girls came here that day. Do you remember that?"

The impatient hand was still and the blue eyes lifted sharply to Philip's face.

"She came, yes," Joseph Rubenstein said, and his manner suddenly softened. "She was still a child, but she had a woman's love for gems. She sometimes would come and beg me to show her some. That day she brought a coloured girl whose English was not good, I remember. She wanted me to show them some stones."

"And did you?"

"Yes." His eyes misted a second. "I almost sent her away. I am glad I did not. I never saw her again."

There was a little silence. "Was there another girl with Shirley and the African girl?"

"Yes."

Philip leaned forward slightly, anxiously. "Mr Rubenstein, if we could show you a photograph of the other girl, would you remember her?"

He frowned. "I think so. Mr Blair,

166

if there is a chance my granddaughter was murdered, as obviously you are suggesting, why are *you* asking me these questions? Why are the police not asking them?"

"The police see no reason to suspect foul play in your granddaughter's death. They have no patience with my doubts." He paused, and added, "Mr Rubenstein, believe me, I hope there was no foul play. I think it would be very hard on Mrs Philbrook."

"Adelaide?" He shrugged. "Oh, quite. Murder is much too vulgar. It's not the sort of thing that should happen in Adelaide's family." He shrugged again. "No, I am being unkind. She was fond of the child. Shirley's death was a terrible blow. Yes, that is true. Adelaide must be a very lonely woman."

"Does her brother live in the house?" Penny asked. "He'd be company for her."

"William?" Joseph Rubenstein made a small contemptuous sound. "You've met William?"

"Yes."

"Then you know the sort of company

167

he'd be for a woman of Adelaide's intellect."

The hardness in Rubenstein's voice made Penny instinctively feel a little defensive of William Ford.

"It's sad to see someone handicapped, even though his handicap seems fairly slight. Mrs Philbrook seems very fond of him."

"Ha! Oh, she is. One must always protect poor little brother who is less fortunate than one's self. Oh, yes. She doesn't see poor little brother for what he is and what he would be, whole brain or half a brain. William is a greedy good-for-nothing with a lot more intelligence than he wants anyone to know about."

He noted Penny's startled look and gave a sharp bark of laughter.

"You think I am hard? I've known William a good many years. William is a little simple. And that suits William very well. What better? It is the perfect excuse. People don't expect too much of him. They understand and smile nicely when he gets tired of a job or says it's too hard for him. They're kind when he's out of work. They say, 'poor

William' — never say 'Why doesn't that lazy bludger get work?' Oh, yes, it suits William. He fools Adelaide. He doesn't fool me. He's no good. A no-good is a no-good, whether he's a bit retarded or a professor of philosophy."

He smiled a sardonic smile that pulled his mouth down at one corner.

"Now I have shocked you by being unsympathetic to a man with a handicap. What about you, Mr Blair? You are blind, are you not?"

"Yes," Philip said.

"Do you trade on your handicap, eh? Do you make others your servants? I do not think so. A handicap does not suit you, and so you fight it. A handicap suits William Ford and so he uses it. He has enough intelligence to know he has some brain damage — and he has; it is genuine. But William is not as simple as he would have us all believe. What did you think of him, eh?"

"He seemed uneasy about us at first, because he thought we were police," Penny said cautiously. "He relaxed when he found we weren't, but he didn't have much to say and left the room after a while. We didn't have much chance to form an opinion."

Joseph Rubenstein made a snorting noise. "It wouldn't be the first time he'd had trouble with the police."

Philip asked, "Does he have a job at the moment?"

Rubenstein shrugged. "I don't know. It might be anything by now; or more likely nothing. Delivering bread one week, City Council road-gang labourer the next, school janitor's off-sider the next. If his sister didn't have money, you'd be surprised how William could keep a job."

Philip said casually, "I suppose you haven't seen him since your grand-daughter's funeral. Did he have a job then?"

"No."

The old man stopped and wiped a hand across his face as if his outburst against his step-son had wearied him.

"We waste time. You wish to ask more questions?"

"If we bring a photograph of Linda Benmore, would you be so kind as to look at it and tell us whether she was

170

with Shirley the day they came to see the gems?"

"Yes, yes." He stood up, dismissingly. "I agreed to see you, and I have talked with you, for one reason."

His face was suddenly grey and strained. "I am an old man and when Shirley died I would not look where my intelligence pointed. That is why I have talked too much about William: it stopped me from thinking, or from facing my thoughts. But Shirley did not go fishing, Mr Blair. She hated fishing. I think I have always known my granddaughter did not die by accident."

9

"AND where," asked Penny when she pulled up outside Philip's flat after a drive back from the inner city during which they had been almost completely silent, "does that leave us?"

Philip's face was so intent she could almost feel him thinking furiously.

He turned his head slowly toward her. "Pen," he said very gravely, "if Joseph Rubenstein knew his granddaughter as well as he believes, it leaves us with a double murder."

She frowned. "*If* he knew her as well as he believes. And — though how it fits in with Linda's death I can't see — we have our first suspect."

"What?"

"Well, don't tell me you didn't think of William. That's why you asked whether he was working at the time Shirley died. And he wasn't, which means he could have done it and no one would have noticed his temporary absence. It would mean there was a side to William no one knows about. It would mean that — far from being, as Mr Rubenstein thinks, better than he seems — he is far worse than anyone has guessed."

"And if Linda had met him and knew him as Shirley's uncle, she might have been ready to trust him."

"But the girls didn't know each other well. I must admit it's a bit hard to see just how William could come into the picture."

He nodded after a moment. "Well, let's keep open minds about William. After all, just because he doesn't have nice manners and a steady job, he's not necessarily homicidal. Let's go and ask the Benmores if they would lend us a photograph of Linda to show Mr Rubenstein. And I'll plague poor old Des again to find out whether William is on record, which seems probable from what his step-father said; and if so, for what."

"When do you want to see the Benmores?"

"Now, if you can spare the time."

She glanced at her watch. "I doubt if

Mr Benmore would be home from work yet — it's only five — but I can come back later if you like. I don't think we should talk to Mrs Benmore alone. She's still too distressed."

He nodded, and sat quite still for some seconds. "If I make it plain it's strictly on a business basis and not a reluctant attempt at a courtesy I don't possess, will you come in and let me cook dinner for you? I don't feel it's fair to let you drive all the way home and back, and I really cook passably well. And I'd rather like to show off my skill to someone."

It can be lonely in the dark.

Penny didn't know where the phrase came from, but it leapt into her mind as sharply as if Philip had spoken the words. And the memory of the other night and his abrupt, almost curt, invitation to coffee came back and she wondered suddenly whether the curtness had been simply the reluctance of a fiercely independent man to admit even to himself a need for company.

Any company, she thought wryly: even mine.

She said easily, "I guess if you can eat

it, boy, I can. Thanks, Philip."

They chatted comfortably while he prepared a meal with a careful dexterity which impressed her considerably, and she told him so. He grinned and told her as a reward for her manners he would allow her to do the washing-up while he telephoned Des.

"Shall I look up his number?"

He shook his head. "That's one of the things you learn to do — memorise phone numbers. I can rattle off about thirty of 'em, from yours to the butcher's. I used to dial the devil of a lot of wrong numbers — get one figure wrong and the whole thing goes crazy, like with touch typing. But now, several phone-bills sadder and wiser, I'm much more adept."

Des cheerfully agreed to check William Ford's police record, if any. "Who the heck," he asked, "is William Ford, anyway? What are you doing there, Phil — starting up a full-scale detective agency?"

Philip told him of their meeting with Joseph Rubenstein. In the silence at the other end of the line he felt that for the first time he had Des' full attention.

"I — see," the big policeman said slowly. "You know, Phil, I really do begin to wonder whether you're as far off-beam as the homicide boys think. I really do begin to wonder."

★ ★ ★

At the Benmores' home Penny and Philip were again met by Ken Benmore's quiet anxiety to help, and his wife's equally quiet hopelessness.

They readily produced a carefully-posed studio photograph of Linda. "We'd like you to take good care of it," was all her mother commented. She had taken the photograph off the top of the piano and handed it quickly to Penny without even glancing at it, as if she didn't want to see it and would be almost glad to have it taken away temporarily.

"We'll look after it," Philip promised. "Mrs Benmore, I'm sorry to go over it, but do you remember if Linda spoke of anything unusual happening that day of the Guide rally?"

Joan Benmore shook her head and her

husband said a little sharply, "She was full of talk of things that happened that day. In what way unusual?"

"I don't know," Philip admitted. "But if it had been anything such as I had in mind, you'd remember. Do you recall if she said anything about visiting a jeweller's?"

Both the Benmores looked puzzled. "Why would Linda go to a jeweller's?"

"She might have, if she went with Shirley Philbrook. Shirley's grandfather is a gem-merchant."

The Benmores looked at each other.

Mrs Benmore said slowly, "I remember she said they'd been to the Museum. If she'd talked about gems I wouldn't have noticed; I'd have thought it was something connected with the Museum. I was sick with 'flu," she added. "I — didn't take all that much notice." Her voice shook a little.

Ken Benmore went with them to the front door, and as he opened it to the cool night he said in a low, hard voice:

"There's a lot we can't help you with, Mr Blair. But there's one thing I do know, like I told the police: whoever killed Linda was someone she knew, someone she trusted. She'd never have gone with him, otherwise."

"Yes," Philip said, feeling the inadequacy of words.

"It gets you after a while, you know," Ken Benmore went on. "You start looking at your friends, because you know one of them is no friend. Someone who held out his hand and said we had his sympathy. And because you don't want to talk with a fiend, you avoid them all. Because you won't rub shoulders with a murderer, you shut everyone out. Maybe it's wrong, but you do it. It's taking Joan apart, this not trusting anyone. It's — "

He stopped and shook his head and his openly honest face crumpled with pain.

"Do you believe in hanging?"

"No," Philip said quietly.

"No." Ken Benmore nodded. "No more did I. But I do now, Mr Blair. I do now."

Penny put her hand for a moment on his arm. "You know, Mr Benmore, it really might not be someone you know. It could be someone Linda knew from school, or Guides or somewhere.

Maybe — maybe the older brother of one of her school-friends, or someone like that. She'd have been ready to trust someone like that. You might never have set eyes on the man."

* * *

Philip was sitting at his desk as his Grade Twelve history class came in after lunch, thinking more of the coming visit to Joseph Rubenstein than of his surroundings, when something snapped him to attention.

"Would the last five boys to come in come back to my desk, please?"

There was a moment's surprised stillness, and then footsteps.

"Fine," Philip said. "Now, I want each of you to take one of these books" — drawing a small pile on his desk close to him — "all dealing differently with aspects of the causes or effects of World War I. This day next week I want you to bring back what you consider the most important observation of the author you've read, and we'll open discussion on it."

He had intended, in fact, to do something like this, but not quite in the same manner.

"Random choice of readers seems fair to me," he added. "Now as you step forward in turn to take a book, please identify yourselves."

When the third boy stepped up and said, "James Taylor, sir," Philip had the answer he wanted.

"Oh, yes, I'd like an extra word about your volume, please, after class."

When after the period the classroom emptied, Philip said, "Close the door, please, Taylor."

"Give me the cigarettes," Philip said quietly, holding out his hand.

"Sir?"

"Don't act innocent, boy. You've been smoking pot. I could smell it when the last group of you came into the room — hence that guff about the books. I wanted to see which of you smelt of it."

There was a long silence. Then Taylor gave a short laugh. "Well, well! Fancy: the wonder-boy himself knows the smell of hashish. Not so staid and sober as one might have thought."

"I don't use it," Philip said. "And what you do outside the grounds of this school is not my business. But nobody will come into my classes drunk or drugged, and you will not smoke that rubbish at St Stephen's. Hand it over."

Taylor put a packet in his hand.

"Thank you." Philip pocketed it. "Now you listen to me. I doubt you need drugs. I think you just feel it's smart to break the law. There may be a few laws which are wrong or ridiculous, and when we find them it is up to us to fight to have them changed. But generally speaking, laws exist to protect us from the harm we may be stupid enough or selfish enough to do ourselves or each other. The law of this State forbids smoking marijuana. Right or wrong, I happen to agree with that law. The human brain is a superb creation. Why knock it silly for kicks?"

He paused a moment. "Never let me find you with that stuff again. And if there are other students who use it, pass the word around. Now get out."

There was a silence. "You mean that's all?" Taylor said incredulously. "All that sermon, and you're not *doing* anything? If you don't report it, and Markham finds out, you're in big trouble."

"If I do report it," Philip retorted, "you're finished at this school. You've a fine mind, Taylor, if only you had a little commonsense. I don't like waste, and kicking you out would be waste. That's the reason I'm going out on a limb for you."

"Yes, sir," Taylor said after a second; and went.

Philip leaned tiredly back in his chair, but he felt mildly elated: he might, he just might, have won a victory.

★ ★ ★

Joseph Rubenstein took the photograph from Penny and leaned back in his chair behind the heavy desk. He looked older and more ill than when they had been there previously.

For a while he studied the photograph, his thin face expressionless, and then he handed it back. "Yes," he said, "she was one of the girls with Shirley that day."

Philip took a long, quick breath in the

manner of someone hit a sudden blow. All the time, he had expected this, and yet when the confirmation came it was still shocking. Someone, carefully and deliberately, had killed two children. He felt Penny beside him shiver slightly with the chill of the knowledge.

Then Joseph Rubenstein's next words hit even harder.

Smiling faintly, the old man said, "Oddly, it is the other one I remember more clearly. Somehow I thought it would be her photograph you would show me. I am glad she, at least, is not dead."

Philip, his voice abruptly so hoarse that he could scarcely pronounce the words, said, "The — other girl?"

"She wore glasses," Mr Rubenstein smiled, "and her eyes fairly danced with excitement when I showed them some stones — indeed, she almost danced. The African girl and this one in the picture, they were not so very interested."

Philip put both hands momentarily to his face as if to shelter for a few seconds from something horrible.

"Mr Rubenstein," he said urgently, "the other girl — the one with glasses — Are you telling us there were *four* girls here that day? Shirley, and the African girl, and Linda — the girl in the photograph — *and another girl*?"

"Yes, that is so."

"She — she wasn't another African girl?"

"No, no." He shook his head impatiently. "She was Australian. She lived in Brisbane somewhere. I remember because she amused me and I talked to her a little."

Philip ran hasty fingers through his hair as if to stir his mind to action, and then could only think of the question he had intended to ask anyway.

"Mr Rubenstein, did anything unusual happen that day?"

The slow, remembering smile vanished from the gem-merchant's face as the grandfather disappeared behind the businessman.

"Unusual, Mr Blair?"

"If your granddaughter was murdered," Philip said bluntly, "it was for a reason. I want to know whether something happened here that day — something the girls may have seen or heard — which might have made someone anxious to silence them."

Joseph Rubenstein's voice was hard. "What sort of thing did you have in mind?"

"Theft, Mr Rubenstein. Or extortion. As a gem-merchant you must at times carry stock of very considerable value. Had the children witnessed a theft or a stand-over threat of the magnitude that might be possible here, the thief or thieves might well have thought murder was worth their while."

There was a brief stillness, broken only by Joseph Rubenstein's suddenly harsh breathing.

"Mr Blair, have you not on several occasions consulted the police about your theories on this case?"

"Yes."

"Why haven't you asked them if there was a theft from my premises?"

"I have."

"Then you know there was no theft."

"I know no theft was reported."

Philip didn't need sight to know that the sparsely-built gem-merchant had leapt violently to his feet. His words came carefully spaced by fury.

"You will explain that, Mr Blair."

"I'm sorry, Mr Rubenstein," Philip said simply. "But it occurred to me that, while you may be the most honest and honourable of men, I simply don't know that. And as a legitimate merchant dealing in precious stones, it would probably be relatively easy for you to do a little unofficial importing as well."

"Smuggling."

"Smuggling. And if a theft of smuggled gems occurred, you could hardly notify the police."

He held up his hand as he heard Rubenstein take a rasping breath to answer him. "Quite frankly, Mr Rubenstein, right now I don't give a damn if you're the biggest diamond-smuggler in the business. It's none of my affair. You may even deal in stolen gems. That, I wouldn't like, but it's nothing when compared with the death of two children."

He paused. "I'm not asking details, and I'm not running to the police, and I'm not accusing you of anything. I simply don't know anything about you — except one thing: you loved Shirley.

Now I ask you that question again: did anything unusual happen here that day?"

There was a long pause. Joseph Rubenstein finally sat down again slowly, and a faint flicker of a smile glinted in his blue eyes.

"I give you one thing, Mr Blair: you have courage — or to put it more directly, effrontery. For a few minutes I wished for nothing in life but to be well enough and strong enough to knock you down. But I think you are honest. I can only add that I am, also. Ask the police. Ask around the jewellery trade."

The harsh, rasping sound had gone from his breathing, but Penny could see it was still laboured and difficult, and ill-health, not anger, was the cause. He took several slow breaths as if to try to fill his struggling lungs.

"There was no theft, Mr Blair," he said, and sat in frowning concentration for a little while. "Nor can I recall anything unusual, anything in the least out of the ordinary. If there was anything, I would tell you."

Philip nodded and stood up, and at once Penny stood beside him and took his arm. At the door Philip stopped abruptly and turned back. Joseph Rubenstein sat in his chair, his face grey and fatigued, his shewd blue eyes on his visitors.

"Mr Rubenstein, I know this is hardly the kind of question one asks. But you must, as I remarked before, carry stock worth a very considerable sum of money. Worth — very roughly — how much?"

Joseph Rubenstein didn't move. "You are quite correct, Mr Blair. That is hardly the kind of question one asks — or answers."

"Damn it, man!" Philip snapped in a flash of anger. "I'm not likely to burgle your safe. You would carry gems worth many thousands of dollars. How many thousand? Twenty? Two hundred?"

Rubenstein shrugged. "It varies, Mr Blair. It fluctuates. But, yes, my safe would usually hold stones worth — shall we say upwards of twenty thousand dollars. But remember: what gems are worth on the legitimate market and what they would bring a thief trying to unload hot material, are two very different things. Besides, outside the trade, few people indeed would know of Joseph Rubenstein or what he does for a living. A thief is not likely to come from within the jewellery trade; and therefore any thief is much more likely to fix his sights on one of the big retail jewellery stores. My premises are an unlikely target."

"They might be more appealing because the big retail places would predictably be equipped with very good security."

Rubenstein smiled. "I have an excellent safe and the premises are equipped with an alarm system which is highly efficient and most sophisticated. These premises would be a bad risk for a thief."

Philip nodded, looking abstracted. "You said stolen gems would bring a thief only a fraction of their actual market value. That would be mainly because they are traceable and so would have to be recut, reset, and so on?"

"Largely because of that, yes."

"What about uncut stones?"

Joseph Rubenstein's eyes narrowed. "That would be different."

"They'd be virtually untraceable?"

"In most cases, yes. If the thief had adequate markets. He would need to know what he was doing."

"As a gem-merchant, you would handle uncut stones?"

"Sometimes." There was caution in every syllable.

Penny was still standing with her hand tucked into the crook of Philip's elbow. He casually let his arm drop to his side, but his fingers found her hand and gripped it with an alerting pressure.

He said bluntly, "Mr Rubenstein, do you now have, or are you expecting in the near future, a particularly large shipment of gems whether cut or uncut?"

Penny saw the muscles in Mr Rubenstein's face twitch slightly. Otherwise he didn't move so much as a finger, but sat looking at Philip with the ghost of a smile giving his mouth a humorous tilt.

"If I were, Mr Blair," he said without hesitation, "I would be foolish to advertise it. My answer is: no. You are free to decide for yourself whether or not it is the truth. And as I told you, I have excellent security. I would not advise anyone to attempt burglary."

Philip gave a suggestion of a bow. "Thank you for the advice. I don't intend burglary. Even though he usually works under cover of darkness, a safe-breaker needs at least a torch-light."

When they were out in the car, he turned urgently to Penny.

"Did he react at the question about a big shipment of stones?"

"He gave just the faintest twitch," Penny told him. "But he might have done that in any case."

Philip gave a crooked grin. "My massive effrontery."

The grin instantly faded. "Three girls, Pen, three local girls. And two of them are dead. Who was the third girl? Dear God in Heaven, *who was the third girl*? How do we find out?"

Penny shivered. "Can it be true, Philip? Is anyone so monstrous as to kill three children for money?"

He slowly shook his head. "I don't know, Penny. But I know this: if that third girl were my daughter, I would get her out of this country tomorrow, and I wouldn't let her out of my sight until then."

For a time they just went on sitting silently in the car, until Penny said wryly, "We'd better move out of here or Mr Rubenstein will have us arrested on suspicion."

"Damn it, Pen," Philip snapped harshly, not even hearing her, "what *happened* here that day? What in hell could have happened?"

She leaned back in her seat. "Well, it wasn't anything Joseph Rubenstein knows about."

"You believe him?"

"On that count, at least. You said yourself that if the girls were killed because of something they saw or heard, it was something whose significance was lost on them at the time, because they didn't rush home and announce it to their families. If they had, the parents would remember it now, even if they hadn't attached much importance to it at the time. So they didn't witness robbery or extortion."

He sighed. "I suppose. But you just said something interesting: that you believed Mr Rubenstein 'on that count'. On what counts don't you believe him?"

"I should think he overrates his security

at the office. His burglar-alarm system may well be excellent. I hope it is, because his safe, though fairly large, is no bank-vault. I should think it would be reasonably simple to blow."

"Says she, from many a year of safe-cracking experience," he grinned. "All right, on what other grounds do you doubt Joseph's word as a gentleman?"

"I think you hit home with your query on whether he has or is expecting an extra-valuable collection of gems to be residing in that crackable safe."

Philip nodded slowly. "I see."

"Which," she added, "brings me to another question: why on earth did you ask that? If the girls saw something, weeks ago — "

"It occurred to me to wonder whether the reason all this is so puzzling is really very simple: it may be a crime that hasn't happened yet."

She stared at him. "I'm sorry to be dull, but how could the girls have witnessed a crime that hasn't happened?"

"They might have seen preparation of some sort, without understanding its purpose."

Penny considered. "It's possible," she agreed. "But Philip, it's weeks ago — why would the killer wait so long?"

"Maybe *he* hasn't found the other girl, either. That, or it was made to look like an accident, and so we didn't hear about it." He paused. "We haven't heard, have we? There hasn't been another child-murder in the past few weeks — even *before* Linda?"

She blinked in shock at the thought. "I don't recall one. Surely I'd remember? I'll check the papers again. Meanwhile I suppose you could — "

"Ask Des? Poor old Des will be sick of the sight and sound of me. But I'll certainly ask. And I'll ask the inspector, too. I have to talk to him again, Penny. This time he'll certainly listen. Oh, I don't blame him in the least for pushing me off before as a crank with a one-track mind, because I had nothing but theories to offer. But now it's different; now we *know* that two of three girls who were together on that one day died violent deaths. Police aren't fools, and only a fool would ignore the danger-signs."

Penny said quietly, "You think it's a

194

race against the killer to find that third child, don't you?"

He nodded. "Unless we've already lost, and he found her first. If she's alive, he has a big start, but the police can use their resources, have newspapers publish pictures of Shirley and Linda, and ask for any girl who was with them that day to come forward — that sort of thing. They may even, I imagine, find out the name of every Guide who attended that rally. We can't possibly do things like that."

"Want me to take you to see Inspector Batlow now?"

"Please. But Pen — still check back through the newspapers, and not only for a murder. Check for any story, however small, of a girl about that age who died in some kind of accident."

* * *

Inspector Albert Batlow glanced at his sergeant as the police car drew up outside Joseph Rubenstein's offices.

"If this old gentleman is on the level about this photograph, we're not going to get much sleep in the next few days."

"You think there's something in Blair's theory?"

Batlow screwed his mouth at a wry angle. "Let's just say crazier things have been known. We'd better find the other Guide in a hurry."

"But *why*, sir? I mean, why would those girls be killed? What could they have seen or heard that was so important they had to be killed, yet so unimportant they didn't even comment on it at home, apparently?"

Batlow shook his head. "That," he said grimly, "is what I'm still hoping Mr Joseph Rubenstein will tell us."

Rubenstein was reading a letter at his desk when his secretary showed the policemen in. He sat slumped in his chair and Batlow thought how ill he looked. He didn't fail to notice the concern in Mrs Frame's eyes when she looked at her employer.

"Thank you, Mrs Frame." The words came slowly, as if breathing was difficult and the difficulty was carefully concealed. "It's getting late, so please don't wait. I shall close up the office when these officers have finished their business."

As the secretary nodded and withdrew, Joseph Rubenstein gestured to the police to be seated. "Well, gentlemen?"

"We're investigating the murder of Linda Benmore," the inspector told him, and produced the photograph Philip had passed on to him.

"Would you look at that photograph and tell us if you've ever seen that child?"

Rubenstein glanced at it briefly and handed it back. "I really don't know, Inspector."

Batlow stiffened. "I understood you told Mr Philip Blair, barely an hour ago, that this is a photograph of a girl who was here with your granddaughter three days before your granddaughter died."

The old man shrugged. "The over-zealous Mr Blair? Perhaps I did. But he is just an amateur. He is not the police. What one says in answer to his questions does not have to be so carefully chosen."

Batlow frowned. "Are you telling me you don't know whether this girl was here with Shirley Philbrook?"

Rubenstein shrugged again. "She may

have been one of the girls. She may not. I do not know."

The inspector leaned forward and pushed the photograph across the desk again. "Look at the picture carefully, please, Mr Rubenstein. Do you recall how many girls were here the day your granddaughter brought the African Guide to see some of your gems?"

Rubenstein looked up from the photograph. "My mind is not feeble, Inspector, only my body. I recall precisely. My granddaughter had with her one coloured girl and two white girls who, I believe, both lived locally. This may be a photograph of one of those girls. I simply cannot know. I know it is not a photo of one girl, because she wore glasses. The other — I don't know."

The inspector watched him with narrowed eyes for a moment. "Did anything unusual happen while the girls were here?"

"No."

"You didn't receive an unwelcome visitor, for example?"

"No." Rubenstein smiled. "In an establishment like this, one would recall anything unusual. There was nothing."

Batlow fingered the photograph. "Mr Rubenstein, you must have some idea. Does the photograph *resemble* one of the girls?"

The gem-merchant's face was expressionless. "Inspector," he said heavily, "there were four girls — barely more than children — in my office, examining jewels worth some thousands of dollars. I did not know any of those girls except my granddaughter, and as I understand it, the other three were not well known to Shirley. I am not a naturally distrustful man, but I am not a fool, either. I watched the gems, not the girls."

"Then why were you so quick to assure Mr Blair that this was a photograph of one of the girls?" The inspector could not keep an edge of anger out of his tone. "We have wasted valuable time coming here on a wild-goose chase."

"I told you, Inspector. Mr Blair is a private citizen pursuing a theory which I confess I do not really understand and do not particularly wish to. He is not the police. To tell him what he wanted to know seemed to be the simplest way to get him to go away and leave me in peace."

"But what you told him wasn't the truth?"

Rubenstein made a vague gesture. "This photograph may be that of one of the girls. I cannot say it is not. To satisfy Mr Blair, I told him it was; and that may have been the truth."

Inspector Batlow snapped harshly, "Well, was it or wasn't it?"

Rubenstein stood up in a gesture which was clearly dismissing. It was a purely instinctive reaction to his unconscious air of authority that made the policemen stand also.

"I am an old man, and I am tired and I am ill. I watched the gems, not the girls. I do not know."

Outside, the inspector swore savagely, and the sergeant said drily, "Mr Blair says Rubenstein was sure Linda Benmore was one of the Guides in his office that day. Mr Rubenstein says he isn't sure of any such thing. Is Rubenstein making a fool of Blair, or is Blair making fools of us?"

Batlow frowned. "Philip Blair has

succeeded in annoying me considerably with baseless theories. But he is a genuinely worried man who believes we aren't looking at this thing from the right angle. Up till now I've been perfectly convinced he was dramatizing the thing in his own mind, but when he walked in this afternoon and said Linda Benmore had been with Shirley Philbrook at a gem-merchant's office two days before Shirley drowned in admittedly odd circumstances, I began to have a mild panic that maybe his theories weren't so far off-beam. But now what have we got?"

He buckled his seat-belt. "Drive back to the office, Don, while I do some thinking aloud."

He watched the traffic morosely for a minute. "Rubenstein told Philip Blair that Linda had been there. Now he says he has no idea whether she was or not. If she wasn't, we have no occasion to consider Mr Blair's theories any more seriously than we did before. If she was — well, what the hell? What does it signify?"

"Does it have to signify anything?"

201

"No. But I'd have to agree that there then may be too many coincidences to be coincidence."

"I think Mr Rubenstein just fobbed Blair off by telling him the right answer to fit his theories. I don't think he ever thought he'd seen Linda Benmore."

"Perhaps. Or perhaps he really is sure, but he's had time to think, and now he doesn't *want* to be sure. He doesn't want to think his granddaughter may have been murdered, and he's shutting his mind to the possibilities. Or perhaps it's just what he says: he's an old man and he's ill; he watched the gems and paid no attention to the girls as such. He simply doesn't know. But he couldn't be bothered with Philip Blair and told him 'yes' rather than 'I don't know' so as to put an end to questions. And somehow that seems to me the most likely explanation."

"We can call it a day?"

Batlow frowned again and moved in his seat, restlessly. "I think so. There was just something — something stirred in the back of my mind. But I'm damned if I can remember what it was."

10

THE man walked down the footpath of Westport Road like a man coming home late from work, having left a bus at the corner. He had not come on a bus, but a casual observer wouldn't have known that. His hat shadowed his face from the street-lights and the collar of his car-coat was turned up against the chill breeze.

He neither hurried nor loitered, and no one would have given him a second glance. Even if someone had been watching him, they wouldn't have seen the intense watchfulness of the man's eyes, nor the way they lit with a sardonic smile when he saw that Number 28 was in darkness. He didn't so much as turn his head to glance into the garden as he passed Number 24, and without checking stride he turned in at the front gate of Number 28 exactly as if he did it every evening of his life.

He smiled with delight at the

thoughtfulness of the owners of this unpretensious suburban home in having planted golden cypress and azaleas. In their heavy shadow he simply stood and waited where he could watch the front garden of Number 24. If the helpful lady who had answered his telephone enquiry about Guide activities in this suburb had been right, he would not have to wait long. Of course, if Julie Parker's father or mother drove her to Guide meetings, there was probably nothing he could do tonight.

But you never knew when opportunity could arise. The thing was to be ready to grasp it.

★ ★ ★

Inside Number 24 a tall man glanced up from the television set as his daughter came through the loungeroom in her Guide uniform calling, "Mum, did you see where Benny put my coat? He was playing at stealing it before he went to bed."

The man said, "Julie, hadn't I better drive you to Guides? You'll be late at the Robinsons. Ring and tell Mr Robinson."

"Oh, it's all right, Dad," she told him cheerfully. "Mr Robinson's never ready to go on time anyway. Besides, you'll miss the news. I've only got to find what Ben did with my coat."

"He put it in the laundry tub," her ten-year-old brother volunteered, rousing himself briefly from a jig-saw puzzle. "It's okay," he added, "the tub was empty. I had a look."

"*After* he put it in, I suppose. Tim, you're hopeless. 'Night, everyone, I'll go out the back door as I pick up the coat."

Mrs Parker came through from the kitchen. "I'll just watch from the front door till she gets to the Robinsons'," she told her husband routinely.

"Aw, Mum, you'd think we lived in the wilds of darkest Africa," Tim protested, leaving his puzzle as the phone rang. "That's probably for me — Jimmy Hicks having homework trouble. Hello," he added, picking up the handset. "Yes, sure. Hey, Mum! It's for you."

Mrs Parker came back from the door

and Tim returned to the puzzle. Edward Parker started to gather his long legs under him to take over his wife's standard watch over Julie as she skipped six doors down the street. The Parkers did not take chances with their children.

But he paused as the television news-reader said: "A section of a Brisbane suburb was evacuated early this evening as a petrol tanker overturned and caught fire. Here is a graphic film report."

Edward Parker stopped to watch the screen.

And in the darkened garden of Number 28 a man's eyes lit as the slim girl came out of the front gate of Number 24 and, pulling on a hooded duffle-coat, turned along the footpath toward him.

He smiled, loving all the world. The people of Westport Street were inside their houses; not a single car had passed since he had been watching, and none was in sight; and, best of all, the Civic Fathers had at some time in the past chosen to beautify the street by planting bauhinias and poincianas along the footpath. Now partly leafless, they nevertheless cast patches of dappled shadow.

Using a golden cypress by the front fence as cover, the man moved swiftly to the front gate, which he had wisely left open. His hands inside the leather driving-gloves were damp with sweat, but it was purely from excitement. His mind was sharply clear and his hands were steady.

The more you read of crime, the more you understood that the criminal most likely to go free was the one who struck boldly and apparently without pattern. He smiled again, measuring distances with concentrated care, alert for approaching headlights. In the morning the papers would say that Julie Parker was a random victim.

Stupid fools. How little they knew how carefully she had been chosen!

He would let her pass. Two steps past the gate. Then he would call her name, softly, and naturally she would stop and turn enquiringly as he stepped up to her. It would be over before she knew what was happening. A hand over her mouth, a quick jerk to drag her into the shadow of the cypress — and then it didn't matter how many cars came down the street. Or a pedestrian could walk by on the other side of the fence, and never know.

He watched, almost counting her quick, untroubled steps. About eight to the gate, then two past. He moistened his lips with a quick tongue.

And a big black dog with some retriever in his family hurled himself in an obviously practised leap over the fence of Number 24 and raced, barking gleefully, after his young mistress.

Julie wheeled around. "Joss, you monster! Who let you out? Oh, dash, I suppose I forgot to shut the laundry door. Come on, I'd better take you home. You can't come to Guides — they don't have boys, anyway." She chuckled.

The front door of Number 26 opened and a woman said, "That your dog barking, Julie?"

"Yes, Mrs Hicks. He got out and wants to follow me. I'm just taking him back."

"I thought we must have burglars or something." Mrs Hicks laughed good-humouredly. "On your way to Guides?"

"Yes, and I'm late already and now I've got to take Joss back. Oh-oh, I've kept Mr Robinson — he's coming looking for me. Jill must have been ready on time for once. I'll have to fly."

She ran back, the dog beside her, and in a moment was out again and climbing into the blue car that had turned around and stopped by her front gate.

The man stood very still in the shadow. He stood there for quite a long time after the blue car had pulled away, taking Julie Parker with it. Stunning disappointment swept over him, leaving him feeling as he had once as a child when a sudden big wave had reared up out of a normal surf, bowled him over and over, slammed him on to the beach and then rolled out, leaving him bruised and shocked and with the breath knocked agonizingly out of his body.

Presently, stiffly, he stirred himself and went out on to the footpath to walk back the way he had come.

What a blinding, rotten piece of luck! When fortune had played into his hands so superbly, to be frustrated at the last second was hard to take. He thrust his hands angrily into the pockets of his jacket. It would be another week before she was likely to be out at night again; he couldn't wait another week.

He could try by day, but the risks were high, especially as this one didn't know him like the others had. He glanced back once at the house. If he'd waited, he could have found out which was her room, though a break-and-enter was the last thing he wanted to try — far too risky, especially with that noisy damned dog around. He'd have to do some more thinking, more planning.

He frowned. He was a patient man, but his patience was running out. He couldn't wait much longer.

★ ★ ★

Des Maddock leaned back in his chair with a lazy indolence that was denied by the alert look in his blue eyes, and by his professional reputation.

"I've a confession to make, Phil." He smiled, watching the dark, intent face opposite. "You'll probably feel like punching my unquestionably handsome nose for it, but since I have such an unfair advantage in the fisticuffs department, I'll risk it."

"Rotten coward. Go on."

"When you first started chasing up this theory of yours that your waitress friend really knew something, I tagged along with the big inside-information bit for one reason and one reason only."

"Poor fellow's blind — only decent to humour him," Philip said drily.

Des blinked. "Did I make it that obvious?"

"Everyone made it that obvious. Most still do. But I wasn't going to let that stop me from using you to the limits of your good nature to find out unofficial police attitudes on the case. So don't apologize. And I really can't blame anyone for thinking I was crazy."

Des said quietly, "Did Penny think so?"

"At first, yes. Not now. Or not entirely."

"Did you mind very much that I sent her?"

Philip considered. "My first reaction was to mind like the very devil. But I

211

needed the use of a pair of eyes; and as she said herself, two years is a long time. One gets over emotional things."

Des studied him thoughtfully. "Penny's got over you?"

"Oh, quite."

"And you? You've got over Penny?"

Philip made an impatient gesture. "I live in a different world, Des. I'm trying to make a living, trying to run a flat. Every corner of my life is filled with just the ordinary business of living. There's no room for other people."

He paused, and shrugged. "Anyway, it's finished. You said you thought at first I was off-beam in this Linda Benmore case. Do I take it you've changed your mind?"

"Well, you may still be wrong, but let's say I would no longer lay a bet on it, and I'm a guy who likes a gamble now and then. And I might add that I have a distinct suspicion even the homicide boys are not just as sceptical as they were."

"Since they interviewed Joseph Rubenstein?"

"Rubenstein?" The big policeman shook his head. "He told them he couldn't identify Linda as one of the girls who'd been in the shop."

"He *what*?" Philip shot out of his chair to stand in front of Des.

"He — well, he said he identified the photo for you to humour you, so you'd go away satisfied and leave him in peace. He didn't want any more questions."

Philip stood quite still for a moment, and then, instinctively putting out a hand behind him to feel for the chair, sat down again.

"I see." He raised his head sharply. "But you said the homicide men were interested. Why? Or are you humouring me still?"

"No. Not any more. Okay, so the link with Mr Rubenstein may be a wipe-out. But that, my boy, was not what you commissioned me to check out for you."

Philip frowned. "William Ford?"

"Uh-huh. Oh, nothing conclusive at all. But interesting, we must admit. Where on earth, by the way, did you dig up Mr William Ford, and how does he fit into this whole thing?"

"We stumbled over him, so to speak.

As I told you, he's Mrs Adelaide Philbrook's brother. Well, he lives at her place, and is a little short-changed mentally."

Des pursed his lips thoughtfully. "So he'd be Shirley Philbrook's uncle, and so would be regarded by her and any of her friends as a person to trust."

"That — plus some sort of mental abnormality — is what made me curious about him. Mr Rubenstein said something which made us suspect William may have some kind of record. I take it he has?"

"He has. It's not sensational, but it's interesting. He went up six months ago on a fairly-vicious-assault charge, and only his solicitor's plea concerning William's slight brain damage got him off with a fine instead of a jail sentence."

"Assault?"

"Oh, nothing to do with child-molestation. But it had a curious aspect when viewed from the present angle. The young man he assaulted was a Scout leader, in uniform. William started picking on him in a milk-bar, sneering at Scouts in general. The man ignored him and then finally told him to grow up and get lost. Whereupon friend William swung a punch that knocked the man down; then he grabbed him and bashed his head on the floor and was kicking him and yelling abuse when several young chaps pulled him off. The Scout leader spent a couple of days in hospital."

Philip said slowly, "And Shirley Philbrook and Linda Benmore were both Guides."

"Yes."

"So one wonders just how bad William's condition really is."

"It mightn't," Des pointed out, "have the least significance."

★ ★ ★

When the doorbell rang again, Philip answered it more or less expecting Penny's voice to greet him. Instead, Robert Henderson said, "Sorry to plague you with school problems out of hours, Philip, but I haven't had a chance to talk privately with you at the school."

"Sounds serious," Philip said cheerfully. "Come in — grab a chair."

"Thanks. I could have phoned, I

suppose." He moved restlessly.

Philip said, "Coffee, Rob? Or a drink?"

"Thanks. Coffee would be fine." He got up and wandered about the flat while Philip made the coffee, and they exchanged small talk.

Philip handed him his coffee and sat down. "What's plaguing you, Rob?"

"I think someone at St Stephen's is smoking marijuana. I've smelt what I think must be pot around the place at odd points."

Philip sat still.

"If I'm right, and Markham finds out, all hell's going to break loose. He'll pull in the police and expel the boy — the whole box and dice. You know what he's like about the school's public image."

"Looking after the school's public image is his job, Robert. But I know what you mean, and what he won't see: the more fuss, the more damage to the school."

"And it's a good school, Philip! It's a damned good school. One or two kids experimenting with pot doesn't mean it's not a good school."

"I agree. But it's got to be stopped, or

it mightn't be a good school for long."

Henderson said unhappily, "It could be one of the teachers."

Philip said crisply, "Why pick me for advice?"

"Philip! You don't think I'm suggesting you might be the one smoking it?"

"Why not me?"

"Because it just doesn't fit. No, that's not why I came. Do you know what marijuana smells like?"

"Yes."

"Well, I thought that perhaps if a couple of us were on the alert we might pick out the culprit or culprits and try scaring sense into them."

Philip smiled. That's Robert, he thought; and the man's concern warmed him.

"How long since you last smelt it?" he asked.

"A week or so."

"Then maybe it's stopped. I confiscated one boy's supply and told him I'd personally wring his neck if it happened again."

"Good Lord!" Robert stared at him. "Who?"

He held up his hand and stood up.

"All right, I know you won't tell me that. I hope he was worth sticking your neck out for."

"They're all worth sticking your neck out for," Philip said.

Robert smiled wryly. "I have some doubts. But I'll tell you one thing, Phil: the school Board were right when they decided to employ you. Markham was wrong."

When Robert had gone, Philip stood smiling to himself for a minute. Then he walked across to his record player, selected a record from the carefully memorized order in the storage cabinet, and put it on the turntable. For the moment he wanted to leave the world and its problems and lose himself in Beethoven's splendours.

It was chill, he reflected. The three-heat radiator stood in its place against the wall. He fitted the plug into the wall socket and switched it on, then reached out to turn the heater slightly toward his easy-chair.

As he touched it, a crashing jolt slammed through his body and lights flared and flickered through his brain.

Caught off-balance, he fell.

As he fell he dragged the heater, gripped in the terrible grip that could not let go, forward with him, jerking the plug from the wall.

Slowly he picked himself up. His right arm, his whole right side, were numb and he was cold with shock. He groped his way to his chair and sank into it for a minute or two. Presently he became aware that the Ninth Symphony was still soaring through the room, and he got up and turned the record-player off.

Then, clumsily because he had to use his left hand, he dialled Penny's number.

"I've just had a shock from a faulty radiator," he told her. "I think everything's okay, but I wonder would you mind coming around in the morning to take the thing to an electrician? I don't want to make a fuss to any of the other people in the flats."

"In the morning nothing," she said firmly. "I'm coming now."

She was at the door in twenty minutes and to his astonishment she had an electrician with her. "Bob and his wife are neighbours of mine," she explained. "So I leaned on him a little to make him come around and take a look in case it's a major wiring fault that could affect other things. Philip, are you sure you don't need a doctor?"

"Of course I'm sure. It just knocked me over."

"Lucky for you it did," Bob told him drily, "or you'd have needed an undertaker rather than a doctor. You copped the full two-forty volts. This cord's had it. Funny, really. It's a pretty new-looking flex but it's hopelessly frayed at both ends. Looks like a mouse has been at it."

When he had gone, Penny turned to Philip.

"Who's been in this flat lately, Philip?"

"Who?" He looked startled. "Why?"

"I've been looking at that radiator cord. I can't help wondering if the mouse who chewed it has only two legs."

"Has only — ?" He laughed. "Oh, come off it, Pen. Who'd fiddle with my electrical appliances?"

"That's what I was wondering. I'm serious, Philip. Who's been in this flat since you used that heater last?"

He sat down, rubbing his right arm. "Oh, Penny — "

"Who, Philip?"

He sighed. "I don't know. I haven't used the heater for several nights — four, I believe. As for who's been in — my cleaning lady, Des, the Walshes from next door — they're often in and out — the man to read the electricity meter, and Robert Henderson. No one else as far as I can recall. But why on earth would anyone want to harm me?"

"Suppose you've got too close for comfort to the truth about Linda's murderer?"

He made a wry face. "That's flattering; but if I've got close enough to scare him, he's the only one who knows it. Certainly *I* don't. And I don't see any of those people as a potential killer."

Penny said slowly, "What about the man who came to read the meter? Did you mean he actually came *in*? Surely the meter's outside?"

"Yes; but he did come in. Something about checking something — I didn't take much notice."

"*Think*, Philip. Was there anything familiar about the voice? *Could* it have been someone you know?"

He shook his head. "I just don't know. Not someone I know well. Anyway, it's silly. It must have been a mouse."

She was silent a minute and then sighed. "All right. I suppose you're right." At the door she turned. "Philip?"

"Yes?"

"Be careful," she said, and went.

★ ★ ★

Penny said brightly into the telephone: "Five Star Bakery? This is Cambridge Fruit Mart."

They won't, she reflected, even wonder whether there's any such place.

"I'm sorry to trouble you, but I believe you recently employed a Mr William Ford as a delivery-van driver. He's applying for a similar position with us and gave us your name as a reference. Would it be possible for you to check on whether he was regarded as a satisfactory employee?"

Please, Penny thought, let me have the

right place this time. If Mr Rubenstein had really meant it when he referred to delivering bread as one of William's many brief jobs.

It was the fourth bakery she had tried. The first had said it was impossible for them to check anyone's record and so it was no use even looking to see if he had ever been employed. The second and third had obligingly checked their records and said they were sorry, but she had been misinformed, as no one of that name had ever worked for them.

The girl at the other end of the line now said wearily that she'd check. Penny waited five minutes before the girl came back to the phone, this time with a hint of amusement in her voice.

"Mr Parkinson says no, he never worked here, but about six months ago he used to collect his wages here, and is that all the reference you want?"

"I see," Penny said thoughtfully. "Thank you — there's just one thing: do you deliver bread to Hank's Milk Bar in Main Road, Walton Hill?"

"Yes," the girl said after a minute, "it's on the list."

"Would that have been on William Ford's run?"

The girl sighed, momentary amusement gone. "I'll check." In a moment she said, "Yes, he did that part of town."

Penny thanked her and hung up, and for a while sat looking at the telephone.

William Ford had delivered bread to the milk-bar where Irene Maxwell had worked, so Irene would have known him a little. He had been unemployed when his niece had drowned and when Linda Benmore had been murdered, so no one would have noticed his absence for a few hours on either day. And if Linda had somehow known he was Shirley's uncle, she might well have accepted a lift from him.

But why? Why would William Ford kill the two children? Neither case had been a sex assault; though it might have been intended. *Could* it be some queerly-twisted vendetta against Guides?

Oh, stop it, Penelope Cosgrove, she told herself sternly. That's crazy.

Then she shivered. Who was to know that William Ford was not crazy? A paranoid schizophrenic could, in his sane periods, look and act like anyone else.

She picked up her handbag and spoke to one of the other pharmacists in the shop. "I'm going out to lunch now, Colin. I might be ten minutes late back."

She took her car and worked her way through the lunch-hour traffic.

The street where Adelaide Philbrook lived was quiet and dignified — almost somnolent in the warm early winter sun. Penny parked her car around the corner from the house and walked back, anxious not to do anything to attract Adelaide Philbrook's attention, should she be at home, although Penny was reasonably confident the dark glasses and rather elegant wide-brimmed hat she was wearing for the purpose of this visit provided fair concealment. She doubted that Mrs Philbrook would recognize her as Philip's companion on the night they had been here, even if they met in the street.

She had tried very hard to recall the car-accommodation in the Philbrook household, but she couldn't. She hoped fervently that it was of the open car-port type, because if it was a lock-up garage she would have no way of finding out what she wanted to know.

And what she wanted to know was whether Adelaide Philbrook owned a white or cream Falcon or Holden sedan. That was the car linked with both Shirley Philbrook's disappearance and Linda Benmore's murder; and if Adelaide owned such a car, William Ford may well have borrowed it.

Penny much doubted if he'd ever have saved enough money to buy his own car, but she had the impression that his sister indulged him readily and wouldn't hesitate to lend him her car.

Penny walked unhurriedly along the footpath, displaying an easy interest in front gardens as she passed so that her scrutiny of the Philbrook allotment would appear casual also. Her heart sank as she came toward the house. It was built on the slope of a hill, low to the ground in front, but high-set at the back, and the drive angled in from a corner of the block, making it clear that the car was garaged under the high part of the house.

And from the street it was impossible

to tell if the car were there or not, or even if there were doors to the garage.

Penny didn't want to appear to hesitate. She put one hand on the low brick fence to steady herself while she shook an imaginary stone from her shoe, her eyes urgently scanning the house.

The front door was closed, as were all the windows. She took a quick breath and made her decision. She would gamble that Adelaide Philbrook was out. Even though that would almost certainly mean the car was also gone, it might give her some sort of clue to both Adelaide's and William's transport arrangements — providing, of course, that she could get access to the garage.

She had put her shoe on and taken one step toward the front gate when the front door opened and Adelaide Philbrook stepped out.

Hoping she hadn't given any visible sign of shock, Penny made what she felt was a fair imitation of continuing an unconcerned walk up the street, taking not the least notice of Mrs Philbrook. Three doors farther up she paused, took out a notebook and pretended to consult it, checking the number of the house as if looking for an address while she covertly watched Mrs Philbrook.

Adelaide made no move to go to the garage, but instead came out to the front gate just as a station-wagon driven by another woman pulled up. Adelaide got in and they drove away.

Penny felt a surge of elation. Adelaide was gone and her car presumably was not. Fate, Penny decided, could not have played more precisely into her hands. She turned purposefully and walked back to the Philbrook house, in at the front gate and around to the back.

Fortune favoured her investigations still. The garage-space was adequate and gave good protection, but there were no doors to block her view of the gleaming white Falcon automatic sedan.

Vaguely aware — without consciously thinking of it — that her actions were not strictly legal and might be said to constitute what the law called being on premises without lawful excuse, she walked into the carport. Certainly she had already identified Mrs Philbrook's car, but something else captured her attention and sent her mind racing back to reports the public had made when Shirley Philbrook had been reported missing, and before her body had been found.

A quite powerful Japanese manufactured motorcycle stood against the wall, a white crash-helmet and goggles dangling from the handlebars. Since it was impossible to imagine Adelaide Philbrook astride any such machine, it obviously was William's.

And one of the reports had claimed that Shirley had ridden pillion on a motor-cycle.

Penny stood quite still, looking at the motor-cycle. A white Falcon sedan and a motor-cycle. It was only coincidence, of course, but it was interesting.

She couldn't have told whether it was some slight sound or the faint shadow-effect of someone stepping into the wide doorway that stood open to the warm sunlight outside. But she knew someone was standing behind her.

She whirled around and stood rigid with shock.

William Ford, a sheath-knife in his hand, was standing six feet away, watching her with a malicious smile.

11

THEY stood as still as figures in a painting for what might have been fifteen seconds, during which time the only thing Penny could think of was that no one knew she was coming here.

It had been entirely her own idea, and like a fool she hadn't told even Philip.

You idiot, she told herself furiously; why didn't it occur to you that William might be at home? Even when you saw the bike it didn't penetrate your thick skull that its owner might be around also. Well, now you'd better think of something to say — and quickly.

The utter stillness, as if the whole world were holding its breath, was unnerving. William didn't move anything except his eyes, and they scanned her carefully from head to foot and back, and it struck Penny that there was more insolence than vacancy in their deliberate stare. She heard again Joseph Rubenstein's voice: "William is a greedy good-for-nothing with a lot more intelligence than he wants anyone to know about."

Whether Joseph was right or wrong, she knew one thing: she was sick with fear of William Ford. She heard a car drive along the street. For the purpose of helping her, it might as well have been a thousand miles away, but at least it was proof there were other humans on the planet. She was not entirely alone with William.

"Good — good morning." She forced a smile.

"Good afternoon," he answered complacently.

"Yes — yes, I suppose it is." She knew she sounded close to panic and she knew that William recognized it.

What am I doing here? she thought frantically; dear Lord, what will I say I'm *doing* here?

"Is — the lady of the house in?"

"No."

He still held the sheath-knife in his right hand, and now he slowly reached into his trouser-pocket with his left hand. As if mesmerized, she watched the almost stealthy movement. Unhurriedly, he produced an apple and began peeling it.

She was aware that he had never taken his eyes off her, and never stopped smiling.

"There's no one but me," he told her. She had no way of knowing whether it was meant to sound as menacing as it did.

"Oh. Well, I must be off, then," she said brightly, and took a step toward the open doorway. William didn't move to let her past.

"What'd you want her for?" he asked, calmly letting the corkscrew-peel of his apple drop on the garage floor.

"Oh, it's nothing important." She knew she had to think of something, though; William, whatever his reasons, was going to make her explain her presence.

"I'm — I'm taking a public-opinion poll." That seemed safe enough. "You know, you pick out houses at random and ask people their ideas on all kinds of things." She felt more confident.

"What kind of things?"

"Well, it can be anything — anything

from what sort of soap you use to how you'd vote if there were an election next week. But" — smiling brightly again and moving toward the doorway another step — "I'll just have to try another house."

William moved fractionally to stand more directly in front of her. He cut a slice off his apple and began munching it.

"You could ask me the questions. I've seen it done on television."

"Oh, but I wouldn't dream of delaying you. I'm sure you're just off to work after lunch."

"There's no hurry. I'll answer." He looked at her empty hands. "Where's your pen and paper?"

"I have them in my handbag." She took out a ball-point pen and the jotter-pad she used for her shopping lists, hoping grimly he wouldn't notice how her hands were shaking.

He leaned forward interestedly to look at the pad.

"There's nothing written in it," he said accusingly.

"Not now. You see, people's answers are confidential — secret. So as I collect each person's answer, I tear out that leaf so the next person won't see it."

"Where do you put the papers?"

"In my briefcase. I keep that in the car," she added quickly. "Now," poising her pen over the blank page and feeling for a panic-stricken second as blank as it was, "first question: are you over twenty-five?"

"Yes."

"Do you approve of the Prime Minister?"

"Only sometimes."

She wrote it down. "Did you vote for the present Government at the last election?"

"Voted informal," William said proudly.

"That's interesting," Penny told him. A sudden idea struck her.

"Do you," she asked carefully, "believe murderers should be hanged?"

William stopped short in the act of cutting off another slice of apple, and for the first time the knowing smile vanished.

"That's got nothing to do with politics," he said sharply. "That's police stuff."

"But I explained we ask questions on

234

all kinds of things," Penny said with a good deal more assurance than she felt. "I'll just put 'no opinion' there, shall I? The next question is about washing-powder, but I don't suppose you know much about that, do you? I mean, it's hardly a man's business, is it? And then it goes on to cosmetics. Well, that's all, really, so if you'll excuse me, I must go. Thank you very much for your help, sir. It was most kind of you to spare the time."

William didn't move as she was forced to step around him to walk out into the driveway. She was thankful he couldn't guess how little her knees felt capable of supporting her on what seemed an interminable journey to the relative security of the street. Every second she expected to hear his step behind her, but when she reached the street and risked a glance back, he was still standing at the entrance to the garage, though he had turned and was watching her.

As she looked back, the insolent grin returned and he called after her:

"How's your blind boyfriend, miss?"

When she got to the car she slammed

and locked the door and sat with sweat-clammy hands gripping the wheel, waiting for her body to stop shaking. Except for the time the doctors had told her Philip might be blinded by his injuries, she had never been so afraid in her life.

★ ★ ★

"And yet," she told Philip that evening, "he didn't do anything. I can't explain why I was so afraid. He's a slightly-retarded person who can't be expected to behave exactly as a normal man would. Allowing for that, there wasn't anything in what he did or said that I could find fault with."

"You had no business," Philip said angrily for the third time, "to go taking such a risk by going there. Damn it, girl, no one even knew where you were!"

"That thought," Penny admitted drily, "kept recurring with unpleasant regularity during my interview with Mr Ford. Anyway, how do we know there was any risk involved? Philip, we can't condemn William before he's had one solitary thing proved against him."

236

"Except that he can be violent and he's damned cunning. He knew all along who you were and he probably knew the public-opinion-poll bit was pure fiction, but he chose to pretend to play along. Why?"

"I think he enjoyed being smarter than I guessed. Oh, I suppose the whole thing was a game to him. But it doesn't explain why I was so scared. It wasn't even the knife. I'd have been just as petrified if he'd been empty-handed, because he's quite a big man and though he looks a bit overweight and softish, I imagine he's very strong."

Philip sat quietly for a minute. "I think," he said presently, "I can probably tell you why you were afraid. You're not afraid of William Ford for anything we know about him, anything concrete. It's the same reason that made me feel sick when you told me what you'd done. He *might* be a psychopathic killer, deadly as a hand-grenade. All you have to do is pull the pin, and no one knows what the pin is. And he might be totally harmless. It's not knowing that's frightening."

"I suppose so. It was finding the car

and the motor-cycle, I guess, that put me in the right frame of mind to be scared."

"A great many men in this city ride motor-cycles or drive white Falcon sedans."

"His voice, Philip — could it have been the voice of the man who picked Linda up?"

He shook his head. "I don't know. I've tried to remember, but I simply don't know."

"He got a very considerable shock when I asked his opinion on capital punishment for murder."

"You're very lucky he didn't give *you* an even bigger shock," Philip said sharply. "Are you tired of living, that you had to stick your neck out that far?"

"Are you going to tell the inspector about the car and motor-cycle coincidences?"

"Says she, changing the subject. No, I can't go to him again unless I've something concrete to tell him."

"Such as if I'd been found dead under Adelaide Philbrook's house."

"Precisely. Having failed to provide any such positive evidence, do you suppose you could go through the newspaper files again and check out those public reports on supposed sightings of Shirley Philbrook?"

She said cheerfully, "It seems the least I can do, having failed to produce evidence that might be regarded as a dead certainty to attract the inspector's notice."

She shivered quickly, and the smile and the banter vanished. "Condemning without trial or not, I do not like thee, Mr Ford. I'm sorry, but there it is and I can't help it. Yet there is one bright spot, if William is the murderer," she added.

"I'm willing to be brightened."

"We can stop worrying about the third girl who was in Mr Rubenstein's shop. She isn't in danger."

Philip shook his head gravely. "Maybe she isn't, Pen. But if it's William Ford we're hunting, it may be that every Guide in Brisbane is in danger — and possibly every Scout as well."

There was a little stillness, a complete silence in which Penny didn't move or speak, and he felt, as he sometimes did, a blazing need that made him want, beyond the level of reasoning, to reach up his hands to his face as if to physically tear away the blanket of darkness. To see, to know what was happening. He hoped she wouldn't notice the sweat that he knew had broken out around the roots of his hair.

Penny said slowly, "I'm frightened, Philip. Call it premonition or over-worked imagination or anything you like. Somewhere out there, unless our guesses are all wrong, there's a man who, whether he's sane or mad, is a ruthless killer who may even enjoy it and there seems a fair chance he hasn't finished killing yet. And all I do is look up newspaper files in my lunch-hour."

★ ★ ★

A bearded fellow-pharmacist came in from the front counter to the dispensary where Penny was busy with prescriptions.

"And what," he asked, "is it this time? Dangerous driving, petty larceny or using improper language in a public place?"

She looked up enquiringly.

"An officer of the Law is asking for you — uniformed, large and" he hesitated a second — "rather good-looking, if you happen to fancy that clean-cut type."

She laughed. "Sounds like Des."

He sighed. "You happen to fancy that clean-cut type. Okay, go talk to him and I'll finish these. It's just on your lunch-break, anyway."

Des smiled at her as she went into the front of the shop. "Hi. Pen, I don't want to push in or anything, but I'd like to talk a bit about this thing Phil and you are working at. Any chance you'll have lunch with me?"

"Not a hope unless you'll settle for a sandwich and a takeaway coffee as we walk along the street. I'm scheduled to check newspaper files."

"Cheaper than what I had in mind, anyway."

"Right. With you in five minutes."

As they walked through the jostling lunch-hour crowds, Penny asked, "Have you got anything for us, Des?"

He shook his head. "I'm not likely to get much, Pen — not my department. It's more the other way around, actually.

I'm wondering what you and Phil have got."

She looked at him in quick surprise. "Nothing sensational we're holding out on. Des, is that what you wondered?"

"More or less."

"But this is murder! It's police business. And if Philip's idea is right, still one more person at least might be in danger. If he had anything of value to tell, he wouldn't keep it from the police — not in a thing like this."

"Are you sure, Pen? Look," he added quickly as he saw her take a quick, indignant breath, "I'm not being a swine. But I've seen how much this means to Phil. If he could prove his point over a thing like this it would largely remove his feeling of being — well, something less than a man because of the fact Linda Benmore's murderer used his blindness as a shield. That's the way he explained it to me once."

For a moment Penny didn't answer, and when she did she didn't look at Des, but off somewhere into some hurtful distance.

"He's all the man I ever wanted," she said.

She glanced at him with a little smile. "Oh, I know it's not like that for Philip. He quite likes me. That's all."

Des said gently. "I'm sorry. But you see what I mean: it's terribly important to him — quite terribly important. If he feels that, with your help — and mine, in a way — he has some kind of chance of solving a riddle as big as this one — succeeding where men with all their faculties have failed — he might be prepared to take chances for his moment of glory. Sure, I said just now it wasn't my department, but I feel partly responsible because I've done a bit of helping Philip. And I'm still a policeman, and there's a killer loose. We can't afford to have amateurs — *any* amateurs — taking chances. You don't think he might know more than he's told you?"

She shook her head. "No. Philip wouldn't take chances on a child's life, Des."

She told him about her encounter with William Ford, and the car and motor-cycle.

243

"That's why I want to check those newspapers. We want to be sure just what the reports said, because the sight of the car plus the Guide uniform, when Linda was picked up, caused Irene Maxwell to link the two girls — and she'd just been reading the paper's story on Shirley's disappearance. So we have to be sure exactly what the report did say."

Des looked at her thoughtfully, and then nodded. "Right. Fair enough. Want a hand with the checking?"

"Thanks. Des, you're really beginning to think there is more to this whole thing than meets the eye, aren't you?"

He frowned. "It still seems a bit fantastic, but — well, I'm not quite the sceptic I was, I admit. Oh, just let's say your account of your meeting makes me interested in your friendly Mr Ford."

"Look, for goodness sake don't take too much notice of the fact he gave me the creeps. I've got a vivid imagination. You do the afternoon paper, I'll do the morning one."

"You know the date?"

"Shirley was drowned on the first

Monday back at school after the May holidays, so the story of her disappearance was in Tuesday morning's paper — Tuesday the twenty-first."

Presently she raised her head from the paper to look across the table at Des. "That's odd."

He looked up. "What's odd?"

Penny was looking down at the paper with a puzzled frown, and had paused in copying the story into her notebook.

"Irene Maxwell told Philip Linda got into the same kind of car Shirley had been reported in. A white or cream Holden or Falcon. But the report of Shirley's disappearance doesn't mention a white or cream Falcon or Holden."

"Are you sure?"

"I've just read it three times to check. Yet I could have sworn I'd come across a report that *did* mention a white Falcon in connection with Shirley's disappearance. What did the afternoon paper say?"

"Very little. The girl's body had been found by then. Police said there were no suspicious circumstances. I think the paper felt it had been cheated out of a good story and only gave it a paragraph.

A murder was worth half a page, but there wasn't much public interest to be wrung out of an accidental drowning."

"Suppose," Penny said slowly, "that's just what it was: an accident. Suppose we've been chasing shadows, all this time?" She shook her head. "Yet I was sure Irene's story of the white Falcon had been confirmed in Shirley's case."

"I'll check the official police reports, if you like."

"But Irene Maxwell was relying on the paper. Shirley's picture is there, all right, in Guide uniform." She sat looking at it and then glanced at her watch.

Des asked. "Are you to phone Philip at the school?"

She nodded. "I feel as if I'm hitting him. And yet — Well, he might remember the car reference better than I do."

★ ★ ★

When she told Philip he said slowly, "Did you copy the news report exactly, Pen?"

She caught a strained note in his voice, as if concentration were difficult, but she thought it best not to comment. "Verbatim. Want it?"

"Please. Just the bit about reports from people who claimed to have seen Shirley."

"Uh-huh. 'Police radio and television appeals last night brought a wide public response. A motorist told police he gave a lift to a girl hitch-hiker who resembled the missing girl on the Ipswich road about 2 p.m. A railway employee reported a girl he thought may have been Shirley boarding the Sydney express at South Brisbane. A woman who lives in the same street told of seeing a child resembling the missing girl entering a police car yesterday morning. Other reports came from Gympie and the Gold Coast, and an Annerley resident saw a girl answering Shirley's description riding pillion without a crash-helmet on a motor-cycle ridden by a bearded youth. Police say all leads are being checked and appeal for anyone with further information to come forward.' End quote."

"Mmm. Does William sport a beard?"

"No. Might have once, of course, but the Annerley direction is all wrong. And no Falcon or Holden."

"There is, really," Philip said.

"What *are* you — Oh." She sounded crestfallen. "The police car."

"They still use white Falcons, I suppose?"

"Yes. Do you think that thought would have been sharp enough in Irene Maxwell's mind to register if she saw another white Falcon?"

Philip said drily, "Quite, I should think. Irene did not — repeat not — like policemen, and I should think every time she saw a white Falcon she thought of the police. Similarly, 'police car' produced a mental picture of a white Falcon."

Penny said dazedly, "But Philip, that means — that means it all comes to nothing. Whatever Irene Maxwell *thought*, in the end she knew nothing."

"I haven't had time to think that out," Philip admitted. "But after all, if Linda and Shirley were together in Mr Rubenstein's office — "

"If they were. He now denies being able to identify Linda, remember."

"Which," Philip said, "brings us to another interesting point. I phoned

Rubenstein's office, because I wanted to ask him again about that photograph of Linda. Mrs Frame the secretary told me Mr Rubenstein has flown to South Africa for three days on business. Now, when someone says South Africa in the same breath as they use Joseph Rubenstein's name, what do you think of?"

"Diamonds," Penny said promptly.

"Exactly. It also suggests that if anyone wants to crack Mr Rubenstein's safe, the time to do it might be three days from now."

"Back to your crime-that-hasn't-happened-yet theory. But *what* on earth could the girls have seen, in that case? Preparations? What preparations?"

"Someone looking the place over, perhaps. Someone — perhaps someone *they* would know had no business to be there but Mr Rubenstein wouldn't pick — like someone pretending to be the postman who was really the local headmaster."

She sighed faintly. "I've got to go back to work. You don't give up easily, do you?"

"I don't give up because I'm still sure

Irene Maxwell thought in retrospect that she could identify the man who picked Linda up. I will grant you that she could have been wrong. I've got to get back to work, too. God knows if it's worthwhile."

She pricked. "What's wrong, Philip?"

"Oh, nothing. Sorry. Just a blue mood — I shouldn't have said that."

"There *is* something wrong, Philip Blair," she said quietly. "What is it?"

He hesitated. "Just a kick in my ego. I smugly told myself I was winning with young James Taylor, the boy who set out to drive me out of St Stephen's because he regarded me as a crock who couldn't earn my keep. I had all sorts of fine thoughts about what I was doing with Taylor. If I could win with him, I reckoned I'd proved myself."

"He's the one you went out on a limb to protect when you caught him smoking pot? Has he done it again?"

"No," Philip said. "At least, not that I know of. He was picked up last night for the armed hold-up of a service-station. He didn't need the money of course. He just did it for kicks, to show how big he was."

Penny said, "I'm sorry, Philip. But it's his choice, not yours. His failure, not yours. Other people can do only so much for us, and from there on in the decisions are our own."

"But damn it, he had everything going for him!" Philip's voice was harsh with angry frustration. "One of the best brains you'd meet, parents able to ensure his education. So why? Why did it happen? Why couldn't I have picked the danger signs — taken time out to talk to him, find out what was bugging him, why he so badly needed to draw attention to himself?"

"You'd have to know a lot more about his background to know anything about that," Penny said gently. "You simply never had the chance to learn things like that about him — you can't examine in detail every student's home life. And Philip, no matter how clever, or how charming, or whatever, some people are bad. I don't know any other word: just plain bad. There was nothing more you could have done."

He was silent a long minute. "Perhaps. Pen, come around tonight like a good girl. There's something stirring in my poor befuddled brain, but it's just below the surface. Given time to think, I might come up with whatever it is."

★ ★ ★

Philip hadn't begun to prepare his dinner. Since he had come home from work he had been sitting in his easy chair, chin on his hands, trying to concentrate his whole mind, and oblivious of passing time.

Eventually, like a man just waking, he raised his head as if in question.

"My God," he said aloud. "That can't be. That can't be."

He stood up. "But it fits," he went on to the empty room. "It fits too damned well. The one thing — the one great thumping thing that *would* make Irene Maxwell think Linda's pick-up was 'just like that other little girl.' And once she remembered — "

He stopped short and reached for the telephone, feeling the dial and swiftly dialling Penny's number. He waited, mentally begging her to answer.

Because now, unless he was all wrong,

the killer would know he had to move, and quickly.

Penny didn't answer. He hung up and dialled again, carefully, making sure there was no mistake. There was still no answer. Maybe it was because she was on her way over. After all, he'd asked her to come.

He dialled another number. It didn't answer either. He wiped a hand over his face. It might or might not mean the tiger was out after his prey.

His fist clenched on the telephone. If half his mind hadn't been thinking about James Taylor this afternoon he might have seen the truth earlier. And conversely, if half his mind hadn't been full of this whole thing for weeks, he might have taken the time to think more about Taylor, and last night might never have happened.

He shook his head. No use to think like that now.

If Penny was on her way over she might well take longer than usual to come, because it was raining and there'd been some talk of possible black-outs because of an industrial dispute. Driving would be slow and unpleasant.

Nevertheless, he wouldn't wait. Fear was gnawing ruthlessly at his mind as he picked up the phone to call the police.

At that moment his doorbell rang, and he put the phone down with a surge of relief and went to answer the door.

"Penny?" he asked as he turned the knob.

"Nothing so charming, I'm afraid," Des Maddock's cheerful voice said. "Foul weather, isn't it? It's set my rotten sinuses playing up. Phil," he added more seriously, "can you come with me? Penny and I think we're on to something."

12

"**P**ENNY?" Philip said sharply. "You know where she is? I called the flat but she didn't answer."

"Sure I know where she is. She took her car up Mt Coot-tha way to a place I told her about. She's waiting there for me to bring you."

"I see." Philip hesitated. "I'd better get a jacket."

"Sure." Des came into the room while Philip picked up a shower-proof jacket, and they went out together. "Sorry to rush you off with all this mystery, Phil, but I'm sure something's going to happen tonight that'll go a long way toward unravelling this thing."

"Yes," Philip said, running his hands over the car as Des opened the door for him. "Not an official car tonight?"

"Nope. My own little Ford Escort. I'm not on official business."

They pulled away from the kerb.

255

"Time," Philip said, "is running out for the killer."

"That's the way I see it," Des agreed.

He drove for a minute or two in silence, and then he added, "You know, don't you?"

Philip nodded. "Oh, yes, I know. Took me a long time to wake up, though. Too long."

"Afraid so. Why did you come, knowing?"

Philip shrugged. "I hadn't much choice, had I? Even if you were unarmed, and I'm sure you aren't, it would hardly be a fair fight. Besides, it occurs to me that Penny may still be alive."

"Oh, she is." Des sounded amused. "And you plan the big heroic rescue, Phil? Hardly equipped for that, either, are you?"

"You never know," Philip said drily. "People like you who always think in terms of violence don't always make enough allowance for brains."

For a second Des' face darkened in anger, and then he laughed. "Oh, I don't know. I've put a bit of thought into this operation."

256

"Tell me," Philip said. "How high do the stakes have to be to warrant killing two children? Or, to be more precise, three. Who's the third, Des?"

Des stopped at traffic lights. "Her name's Julie Parker. Unfortunately she's proving more difficult than the others. As for the stakes — how'd half a million dollars appeal to you?"

Philip didn't answer for a moment. When he did, he was able to keep his voice level. "Not that much."

Des laughed and moved on with the flow of traffic. "Always the conscientious type, eh? By the way, old chap, how soon did you begin to wake up after Penny made that disastrous phone call at lunch time? You never had a moment's suspicion before, did you?"

"None. I didn't really believe it till you turned up at the flat. Everything pointed that way, but I couldn't believe it. I mean, what's the one thumping coincidence that would leap at Irene Maxwell after reading the newspaper account of Shirley Philbrook's disappearance? She saw Linda getting *into a police car* — 'just like that other little girl.' And who told me the

257

paper said Shirley had been seen entering a 'white Falcon' and carefully didn't tell me that what the paper really said was that one report said she'd gone off in a police car? Good old Des, who'd been such a help. And to whom did I talk about Irene's apparent stumbling on to some evidence? Good old Des, among others. And who have I kept constantly informed of every development? There he was again. And who among policemen might be remembered and readily identified by Irene Maxwell because she would see that distinctive birth-mark on his right cheek as he drew out from the kerb after picking Linda up? Even though Penny remarked that if you wore a beard you'd be insufferably handsome, I haven't seen you for two years, and I'd forgotten that mark."

"And I," Des put in, "have lived with it for so long I forgot it also, that day. Until your charming friend Irene telephoned me and suggested a little remuneration in return for discreetly holding her tongue. When I asked why the hell she picked on me she said it wasn't too hard to find out from my unsuspecting colleagues who was the nice young policeman with the red birth-mark or scar on his face: she wanted to return a sweater he'd left in the milk-bar."

"So you killed her."

"Just a quick knock-out blow and then pushed her out of that window. Wouldn't you?"

Philip didn't answer.

"And then," Des went on, "to cap it all I turned up on your doorstep tonight with a sinus attack and my voice rang a bell."

"That, plus the fact you stuck to my side like a limpet for fear I'd grab the telephone. Hasn't it occurred to you I may have already relayed my suspicions to the police?"

Des shook his head unconcernedly. "You haven't. I watched you angling to get me out of the way so you could use the phone."

"So you've killed three people and you plan to kill three more: Penny, the little girl Julie, and me. What about Joseph Rubenstein?"

"Oh, no. Nothing so crude. In fact, I never intended to harm anyone. But I've spent a very long time planning this job, and it's much too big to let anyone stand in the way."

"How'd you come to pick Rubenstein? Why gems? Surely a bank or a payroll — something that'd yield nice folding cash — would be better?"

"In a way. But security's tougher. It's no job for a loner. Mr Rubenstein's a different kettle of fish. And it's surprising all the tips an alert policeman can pick up."

"Just how," Philip asked, "did those children get in your way? What did they see or hear, that day they visited Joseph Rubenstein's office?"

"They saw me," Des said cheerfully. "There I was, properly attired in the right overalls, driving the right vehicle, passing myself off as a City Council electrical inspector checking out wiring faults. Old Joseph and his stone-wall secretary swallowed it, hook, line, sinker. Then those kids trooped in. The old man's granddaughter and Linda knew me. You see, as a Traffic Branch officer, I often lecture in schools on road safety, besides which I've known the Benmores for years.

I couldn't very well have the girls saying brightly, 'Oh, hello, Sergeant Maddock. Whatever are you doing?' I did some fast talking to stall them — whispered urgently that I was on undercover work because we suspected an attempt may be made at robbery, and would they be awfully good sports and keep mum about it?"

"I see," Philip said slowly. "And they did."

"Yes, but they wouldn't have once the story of the robbery broke, would they? No way. And this particular robbery will make big headlines, I assure you."

They were still in heavy traffic and it was still raining. Philip could hear the squelch of tyres on wet streets.

"What," he asked, "did the girls see you doing?"

Des chuckled. "Putting my toys to work for me, although they didn't understand that part. I've long been a nut on radio-controlled model-aircraft, remember? On the side, I've spent considerable time studying security alarm systems of the type Mr Rubenstein has in his premises. What I was doing that day was setting up a device which, when triggered by remote control the way I handle a model aircraft will shut down the alarm system — something which can only be done from inside. Rubenstein's safe is a cinch for anyone with know-how; it's that damned alarm set-up he relies on, and it's good. No one — but no one — could get in undetected while that's working. With that out of action, the job's easy."

"And he's abroad bringing home a nice new shipment of goodies."

"Uh-huh." Des nodded agreement. "At least half a million in uncut diamonds, plus goodness knows what else, according to reliable sources within the trade. Uncut stuff is easily flogged by a bloke who's prepared to bide his time."

"Which you are."

"Oh, sure. I've spent several years in preliminary studies on this. But, as you said earlier, time's running out. Mr Rubenstein's due back in two or three days, and I've got to be ready to move promptly. He won't keep all that stuff on his premises for any longer than the one night — the night he gets back."

Traffic had thinned appreciably, Philip could tell, and the car was beginning to climb. Des had said Penny had taken her car and gone 'up Mt Coot-tha way'. Perhaps that had been true. Philip fought to block his mind from thinking of her, waiting eagerly wherever Des had told her to wait, watching for them to come, blithely unaware that death was climbing the mountain toward her.

"Being a policeman," Des went on placidly, "has certain advantages."

"Such as having children trust you when you offer them a lift," Philip said, and he couldn't keep the hardness out of his voice.

Des was unruffled. "They were quite flattered, in fact," he agreed. "It's not every day you get a chance to ride in a police car. But what I was really thinking was that you sometimes find yourself — if you keep your wits about you — in a position to — influence people."

"Blackmail's another word."

"But not so nice."

Philip said nothing. He desperately wanted to keep Des relaxed, confident, unhostile. If there was to be any chance, any faint ghost of a chance, it would come only through catching him off-guard.

"There's another aspect," Des went on, pleased with himself and eager to talk about his cleverness. "I'm working it so I'll be doing a traffic-patrol on my bike that night, late — the night Rubenstein gets home. I shall be cruising the area of his office. I'll set off my little device to cut the alarm system and enter the building from the rear to attend to the safe. Should anything go wrong and I'm found on the premises, I was stopped in the street by an anonymous citizen who said there was someone in the Rubenstein building. I should use the radio at that point and inform the powers that be, but I'll say I didn't take it seriously and so didn't follow routine."

The car was definitely climbing now, and the road wound serpentinely. Philip thought the rain had stopped.

"If I'm unseen — and I expect to be — I'll leave with the stuff securely stowed about my person — nobody's going to search me — dispose of the evidence of the radio-controlled device for mucking up alarm systems, which might be traceable to me, and dash for the bike to radio the boys back home that I've found a naughty break-and enter into the premises of one Joseph Rubenstein, Gem Merchant. That," he added, "is insurance just in case, unknown to me, I've been seen hanging around the place. I'm a great believer in insurance."

"It all sounds," Philip said carefully, "rather clever."

"Not bad," Des agreed. "Much more complicated than I could have wished. As I said, it was never my intention to kill anyone."

"But you don't mind doing it."

"Oh, no, not since it's become necessary."

He said it with utter casualness, and Philip thought with a prickling of his scalp: he's mad; my God, he's schizophrenic — sitting here chatting to me as if we were old friends, smiling and happy and dangerous as a ton of dynamite attached to a lit fuse.

There was a silence, and presently

Philip felt the car turn on to gravel road-surface.

"By the way," Des said, "sorry about that radiator of yours, old boy. Thought it really might have finished you; and you were getting just too good at the detective game. Funny, you know, I sent Penny to help you so I could learn from her exactly what you were doing. Part of my insurance cover. But I never really dreamed you'd get anywhere. Once you started nosing around old Mr Rubenstein I really would have preferred to put a stop to it, then and there."

If that radiator had killed me, Philip thought, Penny would have been all right. She wouldn't have gone on with the hunt, and he'd have been satisfied. Why didn't he make a better job of it?

Aloud he said coolly, "Oh, don't mention it. I'd never been electrocuted before, so it all goes down to experience. Bad luck I pulled the plug out as I fell. Where are we, if I'm allowed to ask?"

"Heading for an old quarry on the mountain. That's where Penny's waiting. It's not far from where they found Linda

266

Benmore, so I trust it will be assumed that you and Penny were out sleuthing when misfortune struck."

"I see. May I ask the nature of the misfortune?"

"Penny was driving her car with you as passenger. In turning it at the top of the old quarry, she backed it over the edge. Unpleasant though this mountain mist is, the weather is playing beautifully into my hands. And who's to know you weren't both killed in the accident? It's a long drop."

"Charming," Philip said. "But, while I agree I'm an easy target for a hit on the head, Penny may not be quite so simply caught."

Des chuckled. "Especially if you yell a warning the moment we pull up? Yell all you like. I took the precaution of coming out here with Penny earlier in the evening, and I took the further precaution of handcuffing her to the door-handle of the car."

"You bastard!" The pent-up fury in Philip spat out the words before he could grab hold of his anger and push it back under the cool surface.

But it only seemed to reinforce Des' confidence.

He laughed. "You'll find I've thought of everything well in advance, old boy."

Philip kept silent, desperately trying to think; to keep down the horror of what he had led Penny into, and to think. Somehow, somehow, he had to get Des to unlock Penny's handcuffs.

He said after a while, "A condemned man's traditionally allowed a last request. Am I?"

"Depends, old chap. Happy to oblige if it's not outrageous."

Philip said slowly, dropping false flippancy, "Take the handcuffs off Penny for a minute. I want to — to just hold her in my arms and tell her I've been both ends and the middle of a fool. That I love her and I always have."

He paused and swallowed. "Chap can't do that very well if his girl's manacled to a door-handle."

Des grinned. "Very touching. Okay, I'll surprise you and say yes." There was real amusement in his voice. "But although I realize it's what you had in mind, she isn't going to run away to safety, I assure you."

Fear grabbed freshly at Philip. "What do you mean?"

"Unfortunately there was a little accident when I went to put the handcuffs on her. She tried to bolt then, and fell and broke her ankle."

Philip gripped his hands together to stop himself from trying to smash one fist into the smiling, confident face so near him in the dark. If he tried that, he knew, there would not be even a pretense of hope left.

The car slowed and stopped.

"Well," Des said. "Here we are, and it's stopped raining. Mist's awfully thick, though. Can you manage or shall I help you out?"

"You're too kind," Philip said, opening the door and getting out, leaving the door open.

"Philip!" Penny cried sharply from somewhere close on his left. "Watch him! He means to kill us!"

Philip turned toward the sound of her voice and started forward.

"Too late, my dear," Des told her. "He

269

knows it all. Just stand still, old boy, till I begin to get things organized."

"And just what threat," Philip snapped, "do you have left to hold over me now to make me do anything?"

"Easy," Des said, coming around the front of his own car and past Philip. "You'd like Penny's last minutes to be — shall we say not too unpleasant?"

Philip drew in his breath sharply. He had not guessed that hate could become a physical sensation — a burning, bursting pain that demanded action — violent, savage action against the naked evil of this man. And he stood still, hands at his sides, trying in the blackness to hear exactly what Des was doing.

He heard the door of Penny's car open and guessed it to be about two metres away. He heard Des say, "Now, then, we'll just have you out of there and put you in the driver's seat."

So he had handcuffed her in the back of the car. There was a faint click of a lock, and he heard Penny gasp. "Sorry about that," Des said easily. "Can't help hurting that ankle a bit as I lift you. But you shouldn't have been so naughty in the first place. I won't hurt you any more than I can help, if Phil here behaves himself."

He opened the front door and Penny had to stifle a moan as he put her in behind the wheel.

"Now, then, old boy, just walk around the front of the car, will you? I'll tell you where to go, rather than take your arm to guide you. You've a nasty look about you that gives me the oddest feeling you might chance a karate chop or something. Frightfully embarrassing for me if it happened to come off, even though it wouldn't do you any good in the long run."

"There's something else that might be embarrassing to you when it's found," Philip said.

Please, wind; please, rain, he thought desperately, don't make noises now; I've got to listen harder than I ever listened in my life; I've got to hear him move. And please, God, he's got to take the bait.

"What?" For the first time there was a hint of tension in Des' voice.

"In the pocket of this jacket, which

271

you so kindly allowed me to put on, I carry this."

He pulled out a miniature tape-recorder. "Bless the skill of the Japanese."

And he hurled the recorder into the night, toward where he guessed the quarry-edge to be.

"Every word we spoke in the car is on that tape, Des. And the police are going to go over this area with a fine comb when we're found. They'll play that tape. Interesting, don't you think?"

"Damn you!" Des shouted. Then laughed. "I'll find it in five minutes with this torch, you bloody fool."

"I wonder now," Philip said pleasantly. "It might not be so easy, you know. And I should go and look for it now, if I were you. Once you back the car and our mortal remains into your pet quarry, you're going to have to beat a very hasty retreat. Someone might very well hear the crash, and investigate."

"There's no one for a mile!"

"Nonsense. The place is probably full of courting couples."

Des snorted contempt. "Around an old quarry, on a night like this?"

"Courting couples," Philip said gravely, "turn up in the strangest places."

Des hesitated, and Philip thought: I was right; that coolness of his is as much a front as mine; he's been under the devil of a lot of strain, and he's not all that far from cracking; he's beginning to be unsure.

"All right," Des said contemptuously. "I'll go and get your precious tape. And much good my absence will do you. How far do you think *you* can run in the dark? And even if you try, Penny can't move. So do stay like good children till Uncle Des gets back."

He ran. Philip could hear his footsteps, and then scrambling sounds, and guessed his throw had gone true: over the brink of the quarry.

Wheeling, he half-flung himself back into Des' car, reaching for the bonnet-release, praying it was where he remembered.

It was. He felt the bonnet click unlatched, ran around, lifted it and reached into the engine. His fingers found the distributor and in a moment the rotor-arm was in his hand. He flung it violently away and gently pushed the bonnet closed. It had taken perhaps thirty precious seconds.

Then he faced toward Penny's car.

"Philip!" she gasped.

In three strides his outstretched hand touched the car door.

"Philip!" Penny whispered. "What?"

"Move over, Pen," he whispered back. "Into the passenger seat. Can you?"

"Yes." He heard her panting with the pain of movement, and then he was in the driver's seat, slamming the door and feeling the wheel in his hands.

"Is the key in the ignition?"

"Yes. But Philip — "

"Where? Show me. I've forgotten."

The harsh urgency of his voice made her reach for his hand and put it over the key.

"We're going to drive this thing between us," he told her. "You steer. I'll do the rest."

He thought if he lived to be ten thousand he would remember that she didn't say: we can't.

"Which way's it facing?" he demanded, keeping his voice to murmur-level. "Away from the quarry?"

274

"Yes."

"Thank God. We can drive straight out on to the road?"

"Yes. But Philip, he'll follow us the moment he hears the engine, and we'll never out-pace him!"

"Not after what I just did to his car, he won't follow us. Thank God I used to drive one of those Fords. Where are these light-switches?"

She put his hand on them. "It'll need choke," she whispered. "It'll be cold."

Under her hand his fingers pulled the choke. His feet found the pedals instinctively and he shifted the floor-shift gear-lever into neutral.

"Now," he breathed. "Come on."

He turned the ignition key and the engine coughed and came to life.

"You lovely little motor-car," Philip said.

He heard Des shout as he put the car in gear. "Ready?" he asked Penny.

"Yes." Her voice was small and tight and he could hear her breathing harshly with pain.

"Good girl."

He let out the clutch and the car lurched

forward at his unpractised movements. He heard Penny gasp.

"Sorry, Pen." Don't faint, he begged her mentally; hang on, Penny, please hang on, even for a little while.

"Where are we?" he asked. "How far off the main road?"

"About two kilometres. You can change it into second now."

She managed a smile and he heard it in her voice: "That's better. You're learning. Stay in second for a while. I'm not sure I can handle fast cornering."

"You're terrific. Penny, this damned track's so rough — I know it must hurt like hell; but you've got to stand it. It's our only hope."

"Anything's better than having Des catch up with us."

There was horror in her voice, and Philip said sharply, "How did you come to break your ankle?"

"I'm — pretty dumb. I didn't wake up to him till we got here."

The jerky words and her uneven breathing told him she was in agony.

"I — just followed him. Lamb to the slaughter. At the last second, when he produced the handcuffs, the penny dropped. I tried to bolt for it. He — caught me."

She paused. "A shade more accelerator — there's a hill — too much — right."

"And?" Philip said.

"I don't want to remember."

"Penny! Did he do that — deliberately?"

He felt her shudder. "Ease up — we're at the top of the hill. Fog's so thick — "

Her voice trailed off.

"Penny!" he cried desperately.

"I'm sorry, Philip." It was barely more than a whisper. "We've got — to stop. I can't — "

"Hang on, Pen! A little while, please!"

The car hit a pot-hole and he felt it lurch across the road as Penny slumped unconscious against him. Even as he shifted his foot to the brake pedal the car hit an embankment with a grating crunch of metal that flung him hard forward in the seat-belt a merciful instinct had caused him to buckle on.

In a few seconds he became dazedly aware that the car had stopped, tilted sideways in a gutter. He groped for the ignition key and switched it off.

"Penny?" His hands found her slumped against the door.

She moaned as he drew her against him. For what seemed an age he sat holding her, willing her to be all right, to come to consciousness.

Later, he guessed it must have been no more than a minute before he realized Des would probably have heard the crash, and even now he would be running down the road toward them.

Philip remembered the tone of Penny's voice as she said: "Anything's better than having Des catch up with us."

He thought desperately. In the darkness and the mist, he and Des would be on even terms at last. Then even as he thought it, he remembered Des had spoken of having a torch, and in the same moment he thought of the headlights of Penny's car — still on, signalling their whereabouts, for all he knew. He found the switch and turned it off.

How long did they have? How far had they come along this track? A kilometre? Hardly. Perhaps no more than half. And Des Maddock was fit and strong.

A weapon. Something to use for a weapon. But what use was a spanner in the dark against, probably, a gun in the hand of a man with a torch?

Suddenly Philip caught his breath. Snatching the keys from the ignition he pushed open the door and scrambled out. Swiftly he went to the back of the car, his hands sliding guidingly over the body, feeling for the lock of the boot, fumbling to put in the key. Wrong key. The other — hurry. But steady it, don't drop the keys.

Please, God, don't let the impact have jammed the boot. In there is the only weapon we have.

The key fitted and turned the lock. The boot-lid didn't move. Sweat trickling down his face in the cold dampness, he got his fingernails under the edge of the lid and tugged desperately, hearing what sounded like footsteps pounding down the road, until he realized it was the thumping of his own heart pulsing in his ears.

The boot-lid remained immovable.

13

IN the living-room of the Parker house, the television set was telling the evening news of the world's disasters. Julie, helping her ten-year-old brother with his jigsaw puzzle, was paying little attention until the good-looking young news-reader said:

"Would all Girl Guides pay attention, please?"

Instinctively, she did.

"Police investigating the murder of Linda Benmore, whose body was found in bush on the outskirts of Brisbane last month, have issued photographs of the dead girl and another Guide, Shirley Philbrook, who was drowned a fortnight earlier. It is believed that these two girls and another local Guide acted as hostesses to a visiting African Guide as part of special arrangements to entertain the visitors at a rally on May sixteen. Police are extremely anxious to contact the third girl who acted as joint hostess with Shirley and Linda on that day.

"Would anyone recognizing these photographs and knowing the identity of the third Brisbane Guide please telephone Inspector A. Batlow of the homicide division, or their local police station? The matter is very urgent. We repeat — "

Julie, a puzzled frown crinkling her forehead, looked at her father.

"They're dead," she said in a baffled tone.

"Who?" her father asked absently.

"Those two girls — Shirley and Linda."

He turned his head quickly to look at her. "Did you know them?"

Julie nodded. "I only saw them that day."

Her father sat sharply upright. He had no idea what the police message meant, but he felt a strange sensation of intense uneasiness. "Do you know who went with them that day?"

"Yes, of course," Julie said. "I did."

* * *

Philip felt in his pockets for a pen-knife — anything that he might use to try to lever the boot-lid open. There was nothing. He felt for the key again, to try again to make sure the lock had really turned.

And suddenly he wanted to laugh hysterically at his own stupidity. To open this boot you had to first turn the key and then push the latch-button. He pushed it, and the lid opened obediently.

His hands were starting to shake and he told himself: stop it. Panic almost floored you just now by stopping you from thinking; so think, and get a hold of yourself.

He groped in the boot and felt the cold metal of a jerrican, and lifted it out, gratified for the weight: it must be full — two gallons of petrol. He unscrewed the cap and sniffed the sharp fumes for confirmation.

He carried the can back down the road, carefully counting his paces, feeling the rough gravel surface under his feet: thirteen, fourteen, fifteen. He stopped, put the can down carefully and got down on his hands and knees, groping the width of the road from gutter to gutter. A narrow track, seldom used, because there was grass growing between the wheel-tracks. He wished it had been the hard surface of bitumen, but he was grateful for its narrowness.

Carefully he poured petrol in a swathe across the road till the can was, he guessed, about three-parts empty. Then, carrying the can, he hurried back, feeling for the car and finding it by cracking his shin on the rear bumper.

He pulled off one shoe and removed his sock, soaked it with petrol and stuffed it partly into the quarter-full jerrican. His mind full of another desperate prayer, he felt again for the front door.

"Philip?" Penny asked weakly.

"Pen!" He slid behind the wheel and reached out his hand and found hers.

"I'm — sorry," she said. "Rotten driver, aren't I?"

"The best," he said. "Penny — "

"Have I wrecked it?"

He nodded. "Afraid so. Not badly, but enough. Penny, listen. Do you still smoke?"

"Hardly ever. I don't need a cigarette."

"Matches, Penny, or a lighter. Have you got any?"

She heard the horror-hounded tenseness in his voice and it cleared some of the pain-fog from her brain.

"In the glove-box."

He heard her open it, and she put a small metal object in his hand.

He clicked the button. "Does it work?"

"Beautifully. Put it *out*, Phil — I smell petrol."

"You," he told her, "are the most wonderful girl I've ever been in a car-smash with."

"Thank you, kind sir," she said in a small, game voice. "Philip, what do you want that lighter for?"

"We have a little surprise for Sergeant Maddock, should he come along, and I fear he will. How far did we get?"

She shivered. "Not nearly far enough. Half a kilometre, maybe. What a spineless thing I am, to faint like that."

He touched her arm. "Never say things like that about the girl I love. Penny, I think he'll be following us on foot. Is it very dark?"

"As the inside of a black cat."

"Then he'll have to use the flashlight. Can you turn so you can see down the road?"

She moved, gasped at a flare of pain in her ankle, and said, "Yes."

"Right. Now listen. Fifteen paces — that'd be about eleven metres — down the road I have made a petrol-puddle with most of the contents of your spare fuel-can. I have one sock, wet with petrol, stuffed into the partly-empty can, to light with this cigarette-lighter and throw to set the trap alight. It's the crudest Molotov cocktail yet, but it should go. Even if we don't time it exactly right to set the puddle alight, the can itself should help. Can you allow me, say, three seconds to light and throw this thing? To land at his feet? Tell me how far away he is just as I'm ready to throw. I'll have to try to judge direction by hearing."

"I can try. Let's hope I'm better at it than I am at steering cars. Because — Philip!"

Her voice dropped to a tense whisper. "He's coming!"

Philip slid out of the car and stood

partly behind it, can in his right hand, lighter in his left.

Some part of his mind was thinking: what's happened to me that I can throw a petrol-bomb at a man and feel no emotion except a frantic hope it works?

And somewhere in his subconscious he knew the answer.

He could hear the footsteps now, running. He heard them pause a second as the torchlight caught the first glint of the car crumpled against the embankment, and then they came on, faster.

"Thirty metres," Penny said softly. "Light. Throw!"

Every nerve intent on trying to pinpoint the direction of those footsteps, Philip swung his arm back and flung the can underarm. He heard Des say sharply:

"What — ?"

And he heard the can hit the road with a bang and a dull whoosh of mushrooming flame. Des gave a wild shout of sheer fury, and Philip started down the road toward the fire he couldn't see.

"He's run this way!" Penny called. "He's on fire — he's fallen — three steps ahead and a little left. Philip, be careful!"

Philip could feel the heat of the fire on his face, and he could hear Des half-sobbing, "Get it out, get it out!" as he rolled on the wet road.

Philip tugged off his jacket, knowing he was standing above the burning man, and for perhaps a half-second he hesitated.

Then he flung himself on top of the rolling figure, smothering the flame with the jacket, feeling the strength still in the man as he grappled with him.

"Hold still!" he snarled at Des. "Or I can't be sure I've got it out."

The big policeman went suddenly still; too suddenly, and Philip felt himself tense with new fear as in an instant he realized it was a trap. Des Maddock was not badly hurt.

Philip jammed one knee into the small of Des' back, grabbed his right wrist and forced his arm up and behind him, at the same moment groping frantically for the handcuffs, hoping Des still carried them after freeing Penny. He found them and — he never knew how — managed to clip one on Des' right wrist.

And in the instant Des, realizing what was happening, came violently to life.

Twisting his body savagely from side to side he tried to fling Philip off him, while Philip with every ounce of strength battled to hold Des' right arm forced up high behind his shoulders while he tried to grab the other wrist. Somehow he had to get Des' hands manacled. He had to.

And he knew that the big policeman's superior weight and strength would win the fight in probably less than a minute. Grunting and panting with pain and fury, Des fought by the light of the still-burning petrol, while Philip fought in the dark.

Penny shouted: "Philip! His gun! For God's sake get his gun!"

Gun, Philip thought bitterly. How in Heaven's name am I to know where it is? Has he dropped it?

Then suddenly, feeling his grip on the big man slowly being forced loose by Des' sheer strength, he remembered.

When he had last seen a Queensland policeman, they had not carried guns except on emergency duty. Now he recalled having heard the rules had been, controversially, changed.

A pistol would be in a holster at Des' right hip. He tensed his muscles for a fast movement, because he felt that from the moment he released Des' left wrist with his own left hand, he had about ten seconds before Des loosened his grip entirely and flung him aside.

He reached across, felt the leather holster, jerked it unclipped and tore the gun free. He had only once in his life handled a pistol and he had a sickening moment when he wondered whether his left thumb would find the safety-catch. It did, and he jammed the muzzle of the pistol into Des' back.

"Hold still!" he shouted. "Or I'll kill you!"

The big man went still under him, sobbing and cursing incoherently.

Philip could feel sweat trickling down his face and his shirt was clinging wetly to his body. His right hand and arm ached from their dogged grip on Des' right arm, but he kept it pinioned while he tried to steady his exertion-choked breathing. He wondered grimly if he dared try to finish handcuffing Des. Even now he didn't fully trust that he had correctly cocked the pistol, though he tried to tell himself that Des couldn't know there was any doubt of it.

Suddenly he became aware of a sound that was not just the echo of his heart thudding.

A car was coming fast along the bush track. It stopped with a grating of tyres on gravel and two doors were flung open and a man said, "Hell! What's going on?"

"Quickly, oh, please!" Penny's voice begged. "Help my friend. That policeman — he's a fake. He tried to kill us. My friend's blind. Please help him. You must believe me!"

The young man from the car said, "Stay there, Meg." Philip heard footsteps coming toward him. "What the hell's going on?"

"Listen to me, son," Des Maddock said, instantly in control of himself again. He crisply gave his name, rank and number. "I'm a police officer, not a fake, I assure you. Take my gun from this lunatic and help me arrest them both."

"Better tell him not to try it, Des,"
Philip said grimly, or, God help me, I'll
pull this trigger. I mean it," he added to
the young man.

"Why doesn't the lady in the car lend
a hand if you're blind?" the new arrival
demanded.

"Because this charming police officer
broke her ankle so she couldn't run
away," Philip said.

Philip felt a sharp breeze as if
something had brushed close by his
face.

"You really are blind! Hang on, I'll
clip the handcuffs on his other wrist."
There was a metallic click. "There we
are. Always wanted to do that. The fuzz
is all nice and tidy for you."

"Thank you," Philip said very quietly.
"Do you know how to use a pistol?"

"I was in Vietnam," the young man
said laconically.

Philip stood up and held out Des' gun.
Then he stumbled away a few paces
and was violently sick on the side of
the road.

"Hey, mister! Are you hurt?"

Philip shook his head. "Just keep that

pistol away from me. I want to kill him. I want to kill him."

★ ★ ★

The girl called Meg took the young man's car and went for help.

It was a strange foursome the police cars converged on a little later. Philip had managed to use his singlet to bind Penny's broken ankle, using a long screwdriver as a makeshift splint, and had helped her to sit with her back against the door and both feet up on the seat in an attempt to ease the pain.

He stood beside the car. "We make," he told her lightly, "a pretty good team. Suppose we make it a permanent arrangement?"

"That," she answered, carefully matching his flippancy because at that moment neither of them dared to be serious, "is the oddest proposal of marriage I've ever said yes to. Let's hope we can do better than we did driving the car."

"Oh, I don't know. Even that didn't work out too badly."

He reached through the window for

her hand and she put it into his, and they stood silent because there were no words for what they had to say.

The young man sat on the road, gun in hand, watching Des Maddock, who had rolled over and sat up, glaring at him.

"Where the hell did you come from anyway?" he growled.

"We were stopped just down the road a bit and we heard the crash and then saw the fire."

"You see?" Philip said to Des. "Courting couples turn up in the strangest places. Thank God."

"I wish," the young man said a little plaintively, "someone would tell me why I'm sitting here holding a gun on the fuzz. I hope, against the time his mates turn up, it's a good story."

★ ★ ★

Inspector Batlow was in the second car to arrive and he spoke briefly first to Penny before the ambulance came and took her away.

Then he looked at Des Maddock for a string of seconds before he spoke. When he did, his tone was coolly impersonal.

"You'll be taken to a doctor for treatment for those burns. I doubt they'll require hospitalization. Then you'll be formally charged on a number of counts, including murder and attempted murder."

"You won't make anything stick!"

The inspector smiled. "Oh, I think we might, you know."

Des swore with savage intensity. "You never would have, but for everything going wrong tonight!"

"Actually, we've been looking for you for the past hour. There's been an all points bulletin out for you."

Philip stared. "How — ?"

"Your very persistence about the gem-merchant and his granddaughter, Mr Blair, eventually made me recall this afternoon that there had been something strange about her post-mortem report, so I looked it up. Her school lunch had been taken out of her satchel and set out on the grass on the river-bank as if she had been eating it. More than half of it was missing. But the post-mortem finding was that she had not eaten since breakfast. At the time we hadn't thought it important; a passing dog, for instance, could have helped himself to the food. But now I did wonder whether perhaps someone *had* stage-managed the setting to make a picture of a school-girl contentedly fishing.

"It was no more than a chance and a slight one but in view of everything else we put out an urgent appeal on the evening news bulletins for any Girl Guide who knew the identity of the third Guide who played hostess to an African visitor with Shirley Philbrook and Linda Benmore, to phone us immediately."

His eyes narrowed as he looked at Des. "The father of a lass named Julie Parker telephoned at once. We talked to Julie, and she told us of meeting you in disguise at Mr Rubenstein's premises. She didn't know you before, but she remembered your name from the other girls talking about it afterwards.

"We sent some fellows around to see what you were doing, and we started looking for you. Why were you so slow to move against Julie Parker, Maddock?"

"I didn't know her name," Des

snapped. "I had to look over the students in nearly every bloody school in Brisbane. I only just found her."

The inspector was wooden-faced. "Take him away," he said.

When the police car had gone and taken Des with it, Philip asked the inspector: "Would it have worked? His scheme for cutting off Rubenstein's alarm system?"

Batlow shrugged. "We won't know till we have it expertly checked. He did study electronics for a couple of years before he joined the force. But even if he'd cut the alarm system, he still had a long gauntlet of risks to run before he made his fortune."

"He'd have killed the other little girl," Philip said.

Batlow nodded. "Undoubtedly. He may be declared criminally insane, though I have some doubts. Unfortunately, there are some people who are simply evil. Now I'm afraid, sir," he added to the young man from the car, "I'll have to ask you and your young lady to come in to headquarters to make statements."

"That's okay," the young man said

cheerfully. "Haven't had so much fun since I coaxed me young brother to jump off the barn roof with a beach umbrella."

"The kindness of the human heart," the inspector said, "is boundless. I'll take you to the hospital, Mr Blair. I imagine you'd like to speak to Miss Cosgrove."

Philip took a long, almost wondering breath. "In the old-fashioned sense," he said, "I've already spoken to her."

The inspector looked briefly puzzled, and then he grinned. "Congratulations," he said, guiding Philip to the car.

Philip paused a moment before he got in.

"Maybe I'm biased," he said, "but in spite of everything it seems to me like a beautiful night."

Inspector Batlow looked back at the scene the police spotlights showed. The last of the petrol fire had flickered out, leaving a shattered can and a black scar on the road. Penny's little Morris tilted its crumpled side against the embankment in the mist, and drizzling rain dripped drearily off leaves.

But the policeman was seeing a small

girl with eyes bright behind dark-rimmed glasses, fondling the ears of a big black dog as she gravely and intelligently told of her visit to the gem merchant's. He smiled.

"Yes, Mr Blair," he said. "It's a beautiful night."

THE END